the
innocence
TREATMENT

the innocence TREATMENT

ARI GOELMAN

ROARING BROOK PRESS · NEW YORK

Text copyright © 2017 by Ari Goelman
Published by Roaring Brook Press
Roaring Brook Press is a division of Holtzbrinck Publishing Holdings Limited Partnership
175 Fifth Avenue, New York, NY 10010
fiercereads.com

Library of Congress Cataloging-in-Publication Data

Names: Goelman, Ari, author.
Title: The Innocence Treatment / Ari Goelman.
Description: First edition. | New York : Roaring Brook Press, 2017 | Summary:
    After sixteen-year-old Lauren Fielding undergoes a procedure to correct a
    unique cognitive disability, her perceptions of reality are challenged as she finds
    herself at the center of a conspiracy involving genetic engineering and
    government secrets.
Identifiers: LCCN 2016047515 (print) | LCCN 2017011056 (ebook) |
    ISBN 9781626728806 (hardcover) | ISBN 9781626728813 (ebook)
Subjects: | CYAC: People with mental disabilities—Fiction. | Genetic
    engineering—Fiction. | Conspiracies—Fiction. | Science fiction.
Classification: LCC PZ7.G5537 In 2017 (print) | LCC PZ7.G5537 (ebook) |
    DDC [Fic]—dc23
LC record available at https://lccn.loc.gov/2016047515

Our books may be purchased in bulk for promotional, educational, or business use. Please
contact your local bookseller or the Macmillan Corporate and Premium Sales Department
at (800) 221-7945 ext. 5442 or by e-mail at MacmillanSpecialMarkets@macmillan.com.

First edition, 2017
Book design by Elizabeth H. Clark
Printed in the United States of America

1 3 5 7 9 10 8 6 4 2

Dedicated to E, M & D

It is better that ten guilty persons escape,
than that one innocent suffer.
—WILLIAM BLACKSTONE (1723–1780)

We are launching a major attack on the Enemy;
let there be no resentment if we bump someone with
an elbow. Better that ten innocent people should suffer
than one spy get away. When you chop wood, chips fly.
—NIKOLAI YEZHOV (1895–1940)

EDITOR'S INTRODUCTION

2031 doesn't seem like that long ago to me. Yet somehow a full decade has gone by since my sister's operation.

A lot has changed since then. In 2031, the United States was still enjoying the lull between the first and second uprisings. A drought was drying out the last of the great western forests, but it would be another two years before the massive wildfires that left millions homeless and sparked the second uprising.

In the meantime, the first uprising had receded into the distance. Back then, we didn't call it the *first* uprising, of course. We just called it "the Emergency." It was supposed to be a onetime event, something that would never happen again. The power grid was back on, more or less. The government was back to functioning, more or less. People bought the best solar panels they could afford, and kept their garages full of fuel for their emergency generators. Aside from that, we mostly pretended that the Emergency had never happened.[1]

My sister wasn't the famous Innocence Girl yet. She was just poor, benighted Lauren Fielding, nervously awaiting the operation that would finally "fix" her. As though she wasn't perfect exactly the way she was.

But that's enough from me. I've pulled this book together to let Lauren tell her own story in her own words.

I hope you find that the following text offers an illuminating portrait of one of the great heroes of our age. Lauren, if you're reading this, I love you.

Dr. E. Sofia Fielding, Ph.D.
London, UK
June 2041

---

[1] This is based on my personal recollection. For a more academic take on the inter-uprising period in the United States, please see Margaret Evans's excellent retrospective, *While Rome Burned* (Cambridge, MA: MIT Press, 2035).

A note on sources: I downloaded the bulk of Lauren's journal entries, along with her therapist transcripts and the two video clips described in the text, from the RIP section of the Swedish website Wiki-Plus. Rather than stick to strict chronological order, I've placed each therapist transcript immediately after the most relevant journal entries.

The final five journal entries are published here for the first time. They came into my possession as handwritten hard copy several years ago. I've since had a panel of independent forensic-document experts verify them to have been written in Lauren's hand.

Aside from the reordering noted above, I've changed nothing substantive in any of the journal entries. I've cleaned up the grammar and spelling and minimized the profanity (for obvious reasons having to do with publication in jurisdictions like the New Confederacy and the Singapore Federation), but that's it. —ESF

JOURNAL OF
LAUREN C. FIELDING

Monday, September 1, 2031

Dear Dr. Corbin,

You said it was really important that I start a journal so you could tell whether my brain starts getting better after the operation tomorrow. The thing is, I have no idea what to write. So I decided I would start by writing you a thank-you note. I hope that's okay.

Thank you soooo much! My father says you're like this super-important scientist, and here you are spending all this time helping me. I never had the guts to tell you this to your face, but you sort of remind me of one of the fairies from the old version of *Sleeping Beauty*. The wise one, I mean—not one of the funny ones who keep bickering over what color Princess Aurora's dress should be. I think her name's Flora.[2]

Have you seen the old 2-D Walt Disney movies, Dr. Corbin? My friends think I'm stupid old-fashioned, but I've watched all the old Disney movies like a million times. I watch new movies with my friends, too, but I don't usually get them. Not really. There's always someone bad pretending to be good or maybe someone who seems mean, but who's actually nice deep down or something. Honestly, most of the movies I see, I don't even try to follow the story. I just look at the clothes. People wear such nice clothes in movies.

But the old Disney movies are easy to understand—even for me. The good guys are good, the bad guys are bad. Sometimes there's something a little tricky, like in *Aladdin* when the bad wizard pretends to be an old man for a little bit, but I can almost always figure those bits out after a few times through.

Sorry if I'm rambling, Dr. Corbin! You said I should talk about what's going on in my head, but all I can think about is what's going to happen tomorrow. And you—of all people—already know about that. My dad said there's no one in the world who knows more about what's wrong with me than you, and that you're the one who figured out that I didn't just have a weird variant of Williams syndrome, like all the other doctors always

---

[2] I believe Lauren means Fauna, the green fairy in the 1959 version of *Sleeping Beauty*. Our parents never allowed her to see the 2023 remake due to its explicit sexual references.

said. So I feel a little dumb telling *you* what's going to happen tomorrow.

But okay. I'm sitting on my bed, talking this into my tablet, and all I'm thinking about is that tomorrow my parents will drive me back to your lab. One of the doctors who works for you is going to give me drugs to make me go to sleep, and then you're going to cut open my head. My skull and everything. You said you're not going to operate on my brain, not exactly, but cutting a little window in my skull seems pretty close, don't you think?

Shoot, Dr. Corbin. I just thought of something. Are you going to have to cut my hair before the operation? I wish I had asked that super-nice orderly—Eric—who showed me around last time I was at your office.

Eric took me to the room where I'll be staying and the room where you'll be doing the operation. He even asked if I wanted to see the tools you were going to use to open me up. He told me you have a special chain saw to cut through my skull, like a smaller version of what my dad would use to cut up a log. (Eric doesn't know my father, or he would know my father has never, in his whole life, cut up a log.) After Eric told me about the chain saw, he laughed and said he was kidding, but I don't know if he was really kidding or if he was just saying he was kidding to make me feel better. I'm really bad at telling stuff like that.

Which is why, even with the whole head-cutting-open thing, I'm super-excited about tomorrow. Because afterward, I won't be stupid anymore. Not that I'm stupid, exactly, but you know what I mean. I'll get when people are joking. I'll be able to . . . what did you call it? Draw inferences. That will be awesome. I love so many people so much—it's going to be amazing to really understand them.

Your friend,

Lauren C. Fielding

CASE NOTES OF
DR. FINLAY BRECHEL

December 2, 2031

The subject, Lauren Fielding, is a sixteen-year-old girl. Skinny, verging on gaunt, but muscular. Postoperative scars still visible through crew-cut hair. A far cry from her preoperative photos three months ago, in which she was a slightly plump redhead with shoulder-length hair, smiling broadly in every picture.

According to her medical chart, she remanded herself to the custody of this facility twenty-three days ago, about two months after being treated here for a preexisting disability. Neither the details of her initial disability, nor the course of treatment, are entirely clear to me, but as far as I can tell, her disability had both cognitive and behavioral components. (Her medical papers repeatedly mention "modified oligodendrocytes"—I have no real idea what that means. I know oligodendrocytes are a type of brain cell that connect different parts of the brain, but I can't imagine that it's possible to deliberately modify such tiny, poorly understood cells. Ah, to be a neuroscientist instead of a humble psychologist . . .)

I have sent Dr. Corbin a note asking for more details regarding Ms. Fielding's treatment and case history, but I'm not entirely sure I'll understand any additional details she provides. It seems to me that Corbin is operating somewhere on the frontiers of brain science with her treatment of Ms. Fielding, while my understanding is stuck in 2024 or so.

What I do know is that Ms. Fielding is currently exhibiting pronounced signs of paranoid delusions. I believe these delusions are responsible for the multiple violent episodes she's initiated since coming to this facility. Due to previous assaults on past therapists and orderlies (including a particularly violent one on the orderly Eric Schafer, who she mentions so favorably in her first journal entry), she is heavily restrained when we meet.

Transcribed from intake interview:

Hello, Lauren. I'm Dr. Brechel. I'm here to—

What's today?

Tuesday. Why do you—

No. The date. What's today's date?

Oh. Ah. December 2.

(silence)

Is there a reason that the date's important to you?

(silence, then a slow, wry nod) Trying to prepare
    myself, I guess. I scheduled my post to go live on
    December 4, so I figure they'll kill me soon after.

Who will kill you?

(shrugs) Dr. Corbin. Paxeon. The Department.
    Anyone who wants the Emergency Act to be
    extended. They're all going to be pretty mad.

Why's that?

I arranged for some things to go public, things that
    I don't think they're going to be very happy
    about. Details about what they did to me.

And what did they do to you?

I don't want to be the person who tells you. You
    seem like a nice guy. I see you're divorced, but
    I'm guessing you have kids, right?

*(Note—I would swear that my face showed nothing
    here, but the subject nodded to herself.)*

Sorry. I couldn't resist. Sasha calls it my Sherlock
    Holmes trick. It was easy—you keep touching
    your ring finger like you're expecting to find a
    ring to fidget with, but there's nothing there.
    The kids were just a guess, but your eyes
    widened a bit when I mentioned them, so I'm
    guessing I was right. No custody, I assume, if

10

you're living at Paxeon, which of course you are, as I don't think anyone could be as clean-shaven as you if they weren't living super-close to where they work, and I know most of the staff here lives on-site. Still, you must care about the kids or you wouldn't have reacted quite so much when I mentioned them.

So, yeah, I'm not going to give you any details. Not today. I don't want to make your kids orphans. If you decide to stick around, you might want to take out some life insurance.

I understand you've attacked a few of your therapists.

Oh, I'm sorry—did you think I was threatening you? How would that work, with me in my ankle cuffs and handcuffs? Believe me, Dr. Brechel, I'm the least of your worries. My advice to you is quit while you can. They'd still let you walk away at this point. Probably. It can't hurt to try.

JOURNAL OF
LAUREN C. FIELDING

Friday, September 26, 2031

Dear Dr. Corbin,

Well, here I am, back at home. It's a beautiful autumn day. The sun is shining, the leaves are changing color, and I'm stuck inside. I wish my head didn't hurt so much. I love walking through the woods on this kind of fall day, with the leaves swirling down around me.

I've been home for a week now, which I guess means it's been more than three weeks since the operation. I don't remember the operation at all. One second I was lying down talking to you while another doctor fiddled with the big drug machine. The next second, I was half-asleep in another room with the world's worst headache.

I didn't totally wake up until like a week after the operation.

I guess you had me on superstrong painkillers so I wouldn't be too uncomfortable while the big cuts on my head healed. Thanks for that! Though—ugh—I have to tell you I freaked when I got my first look in a mirror after the operation. I look like girl Frankenstein, with stitches and metal staples all over my scalp.

That was the worst part of preparing for the operation—when Eric shaved my head. Eric had been super-nice all day, helping me get ready, but it was still hard to sit there in the waiting room and feel the electric razor moving over my scalp.

I had terrific hair. Red, glossy, and down to my shoulders. And now I don't even have a crew cut. Just bandaged skin and a little stubble.

Like I said, I was totally hazy for the first week or so. I sort of remember Eric feeding me and washing me. I *think* I remember you examining me a few times, and I definitely remember when you told my parents they could take me home last week.

Now, three weeks after the operation, my head is finally starting to feel better, but I still get this killer headache when I move too fast or stare at anything for too long. Just talking to my computer for these few minutes has made my head hurt worse. I'll try again tomorrow.

Your friend,

Lauren

CASE NOTES OF
DR. FINLAY BRECHEL

December 3, 2031

Transcribed from interview:

Good morning, Lauren.

What's the date?

December 3.

Any announcements on the Emergency Act being
allowed to expire?

*Nothing that I've seen. Dr. Corbin mentioned that
you're very concerned about the expiry of the
Emergency Act. Tell me about—*

(subject interrupts) I'm concerned? (laughter) I'd
say she was the concerned one. I mean, which of
us has a research project specifically devoted to
extending it?

(more laughter) Sorry. I think they shot me full of
some drug to make me talk to you, and it's
making me laugh more than usual. Or maybe
you're just a lot funnier than those Paxeon
bastards they had in here before. With them, the
drugs just made me want to kick their faces in.

*Yes, I've seen their medical records. You broke
Dr. Meyers's nose and knocked out two of
Dr. Stewart's teeth.*

I'm not a big fan of Paxeon flunkies. I think you and
I will get along fine.

*Just to be clear—I work for Paxeon as much as any
of your former therapists did. As of last week,
I'm a full-time Paxeon employee—Dr. Corbin
insisted that I clear my very busy practice and
focus only on you.*

(laughter) You're no Paxeon flunky. You're not smug
enough, and—no offense—your clothes aren't
expensive enough. That's why I'm worried about
you. Dr. Corbin doesn't strike me as someone
who tolerates a lot of leftovers. Look. If you're
determined to stick around, at the very least
upload your notes to one of the Swedish
platforms. You know, where they'll publish your
blog if you don't log in for a certain number of
days. Just give Paxeon a reason to keep you
alive. That's all I'm saying.

Dr. Corbin has no intention of hurting me, nor of hurting you. On the contrary, she worked very hard to find a therapist she thought could help you. Why would she bring me here to focus exclusively on you if she had any interest in harming you?

Huh. Gee. She must be a saint after all. (laughter) Sorry. Sorry. I'm just imagining nuns lighting candles in front of a picture of Dr. Corbin's evil little face. You know—like one of those paintings where the saint's face has a halo behind it. Saint Patricia of the gigantic bank account.

Hmm. At any rate—if you agree, we'll be meeting twice a day for at least the next month.
Dr. Corbin feels very responsible for your condition, and is sparing no cost to—

(Note—Subject lapsed into hysterical laughter, so much so that I was on the verge of summoning orderlies when she began to calm down.)

Oh my God. I really can't tell—is it the drugs or are you the funniest man I've ever met? If it's the drugs, I totally get why people abuse this stuff. Of course Corbin *feels* responsible! She *is* responsible for my condition.

So you blame Dr. Corbin for your current situation?

Obviously I blame Dr. Corbin. And, hey, you want

to know one reason why Corbin was so keen to find me a therapist I would talk to?

Yes, I do.

Like I told you, I have everything set to be posted online December 4. Tomorrow. All the journal entries that I wrote—the real journal entries, I mean—not the edited crap that I sent Corbin. Plus all the Department memos I stole . . . everything is going to be posted. Corbin must be desperate to keep that from happening. That's why she hired you. To pry the password out of me before it's too late.

I see. You believe Dr. Corbin wants me to insinuate myself into your good graces in the interests of stopping your information from being posted on the Internet.

Exactly.

Which is set to happen tomorrow, correct? So she thought I could somehow divine your password in two days or less?

I didn't tell her exactly when I'd set it to go live. Just early December sometime.

All right. Let me propose an experiment. Don't tell me your password. Let's see what happens tomorrow. If I come back and we continue our conversation as usual, even with your information up on the Internet, then perhaps

we can agree that you've misjudged Dr. Corbin's
intentions.

In the meantime, allow me to help you separate fact
from fiction. I have neither the ability nor the
inclination to somehow ferret information from
you. I'm here to assess the stability of your
condition, help you become conscious of your own
mental state, and ultimately prepare you to
rejoin society.

Oh. Jeez. Really? My mistake. I guess I should just
relax, then, huh?

(long silence)

We'll talk again tomorrow, okay?

Whenever you want, Dr. Brechel. Just keep the
laughs coming.

JOURNAL OF
LAUREN C. FIELDING

Monday, October 6, 2031

Hi Dr. Corbin,

My mom gave me all your messages and told me I had to start writing more journal entries for you so you could tell if I'm getting better. Thanks for checking in on me! I'm sorry I didn't send you anything last week. Honestly, I've been feeling pretty ragged. I'm still not feeling so great, but today my mom let my friends Riley and Gabriella visit, so at least I have something to tell you about.

Riley and Gabriella and I have been best friends since forever. You might even know Riley's father—Blair Halston. My father says you and the rest of the people at Paxeon work really closely with the Department, and Mr. Halston is a super-bigwig at the Department.

Riley walked in and sat on the side of my bed. "Lauren! I can't believe you chopped off all your hair."

"Not me," I said. "The hospital orderly."

"It looks good," Gabriella said. She put a bag full of papers on top of my desk. "You look like a sexy punk."

"Hey, thanks!" Up until then, I'd been thinking I looked horrible.

Gabriella nudged the bag with her foot. "We already have a ton of assignments. I can't believe how much harder eleventh grade is. With college visits and stuff, it's like we have no time for anything but school this year."

"You should have had the operation in May," Riley said. "That way you could have skipped all your finals."

"No," Gabriella said. "They would have made her take finals in July, and she wouldn't have had any summer vacation at all. Anyway, September is always the worst month of school. I wish I got to miss it, too."

My mother swept into the room carrying a vase full of flowers. "Don't be too jealous, girls. Lauren's going to have to make up all the work she misses. These are beautiful, by the way. Look at what your friends brought you, Lauren."

"Thanks guys," I said.

"Riley paid." Gabriella pushed some of my stuffed animals aside and flopped down on my beanbag. "But I helped pick them out."

"I didn't pay," Riley said. "My father put me in touch with a florist friend of his, that's all."

"Tell him thanks," I said. It's great having a friend whose father is high up in the Department. Last year for Riley's birthday, he got the three of us tickets to an FG concert that was sold out months in advance.

Riley shrugged. "Just imagine if you were a friend of Cedar's—your mom would have needed a dozen vases."

(This might make you think Cedar is Riley's brother or something, but Cedar is actually her father's dog—one of those super-fluffy white dogs. A Pomerian, if you know what those look like, Dr. Corbin. Riley is always talking about how her father likes Cedar more than her. By now even *I* know she's joking when she brings it up.)

"Now, Riley—" my mother was saying, when her phone beeped. She looked at it. "Damn," she said. "I have to take this. You girls remember that Lauren had major brain surgery a month ago. No music, no videos, and no loud noises." She opened the door to Evelyn's room, across the hall.

My sister, Evelyn, was sitting at her desk, typing on her computer. Most kids I know just talk their papers into their devices, but Evelyn still keyboards everything. She says it's easier to catch careless mistakes that way. God knows why she cares—mistakes or no mistakes, she'd still be the smartest girl in our high school.

"Evelyn," my mother said. "Did you hear me?"

Evelyn nodded without looking up. "You told them to remember that Lauren just had brain surgery. I don't think they're going to forget. Could you close my door, please?"

"No. I want you to make sure they have a very quiet, mellow visit."

At this, Evelyn did look up. "What? For God's sake, they're sixteen. If you can't trust them, just kick them out."

My mother ignored her, putting on her headset as she walked away from us.

Evelyn sighed and turned to Riley and Gabriella. "You heard her. Keep it down, or I'm throwing you out." She stood and closed the door to her room.

"Hi Evelyn," Riley said to the closed door. "Nice to see you, Evelyn."

Gabriella laughed. Then she asked me, "So did the operation work?"

"I don't know," I said.

"Did you hear that Bea Thomas grew an extra arm?" Riley patted her head. "Straight out the top of her head. It's to help her reach higher shelves in the grocery store."

"No way! That must look so crazy."

Riley frowned. "I don't think the operation helped, Lauren. Beatrice Thomas didn't, you know, really grow a third arm. No one could do that."

"It's okay," Gabriella said to me. "Maybe it'll happen slowly."

I peeked inside the bag of schoolwork that Gabriella had brought home, but just for a second. I'm not starting the makeup work until it stops hurting to read. "So what have I missed?"

"I bombed a trigonometry test," Riley said.

"Me too," Gabriella said. "Trig is a lot harder than geometry."

I frowned. Math has always been like the one class I *don't* need help with. I hope I don't have to start going to tutors for math, too.

"Aside from classes, what's been happening?" I asked.

Gabriella shrugged. "Jacob Kalish started dating Kee Ting Tam.

Oh, and there's this new guy, Sasha, who Riley thinks is hot. He lives right around here, actually."

"Sasha *is* extremely good-looking," Riley said. "There's nothing subjective about it."

"Oh—and oh my God!" Gabriella said. "You missed the whole deal with Dr. Newman."

"Dr. Newman the history teacher?" I asked. My sister, Evelyn, really likes Dr. Newman, but he only teaches honors courses, so I've never had him.

"No," Riley said. "Dr. Newman the sex offender who used to be the history teacher."

"What?!" I said.

Gabriella shook her head, eyes wide. "Principal Abbott had an assembly with the whole school and he almost started crying when he talked about how Newman was a sex offender and we should call the police right away if we ever see him again."

"I heard he abducted Peter . . . ah, what's-his-name?" Riley said.

"Connelly," Gabriella supplied.

"Wait," I said. "Evelyn's friend? Newman abducted Peter? Are you joking again?" Across the hall, Evelyn's door opened a crack.

Riley shook her head. "Nope. That's what I heard. And I haven't seen Peter around for a few days. So it's possible, anyway."

Evelyn's door slammed back shut.

"What?" Riley called across the hallway. "You don't think Peter was abducted?"

Evelyn flung her door all the way open, so abruptly that I

jumped. "Of course I don't think Peter was abducted. At least not by Dr. Newman. Who—by the way—is definitely *not* a sex offender. I think Newman said some things in class that got back to the wrong people."

"The 'wrong people'? Do you mean people who work for the Department?" Riley was smiling as she asked this, so maybe she was joking. "Or, maybe, you think one of the sponsoring corporations had him arrested?"

"Riley!" Gabriella said.

"What?" Riley said. "You're allowed to say anything you want in private, and anyway, my dad says it's not against the Emergency Act if you ask it like a question."

"Your father would know, wouldn't he?" Evelyn said. Riley shut her mouth so suddenly you could hear the click when her teeth banged together. "And no," Evelyn said. "I certainly didn't mean the Department. I would *never* say anything negative about the Department or one of the sponsoring corporations who work so hard to keep us all safe."

By the way, Dr. Corbin, just in case you don't know: when someone mentions the "Department," they almost always mean the United States Department of Security, Defense, and Well-Being. It took me forever to figure that out. I used to get really confused between "the Department" and department stores like Nordstrom and the legal department where my mother works. Why would you use the same word to describe three things that are so different? And why doesn't anyone else find that confusing? Can your operation really help me understand something like that? I sure hope so! Anyway, the Department is the government agency that keeps us safe and makes sure another Emergency doesn't happen.

"So who did you mean?" I asked. "When you said it 'got back to the wrong people'?"

Evelyn stared past me for so long that I looked out my window, too, trying to see what was so interesting. It was a nice day, sunny, with the maple tree in our yard in full autumn colors. But there was nothing happening out there except for a squirrel running down one of the maple's branches.

Do you have squirrels where you live, Dr. Corbin? I don't know what happened, but during the Emergency it was like all the squirrels in Bethesda disappeared for a few years. It's only now we're starting to see them again.[3]

---

[3] What happened, of course, is that people got hungry. Us included. A few weeks after Hurricane Josephine, my mother took nine-year-old Lauren on some made-up errand while my father and I waited in the yard with a .22 rifle. He managed to get three squirrels, still plump with the summer's bounty. We made squirrel-and-potato stew on my parents' old camping stove that evening, and ate well for the first time in a week.

It's funny. The first uprising is generally remembered as a national tragedy, the end of American innocence, etc. But I remember the weeks immediately after Hurricane Josephine fondly. My parents weren't working for once. Every night, with the power dead, they told Lauren and me stories over candlelight. During the days, I'd tramp around the traffic-less roads with my father as he looked for a cell-phone signal. Or walk to the government depot with my mother, charge up our tablets, and drag home our day's allotment of water.

We heard radio reports about riots in the District, and the terrorist attacks on the White House, but we didn't see any violence around us. On the contrary—I never saw people so friendly. We met neighbors we'd never seen before. It wasn't until almost a full month later that things got scary, with people getting arrested and troops everywhere.

"I don't know," she finally said. "People who disagreed with him, I guess."

"So you think that some people said he was a sex offender just because they disagreed with him?"

Evelyn made a funny face, like she had sucked on a lemon or something. "I don't know, Lauren. Let's talk about something else."

"Good idea," Gabriella said. "So Evelyn. What universities are you applying to?"

Evelyn blinked a few times. "I'm not sure," she said finally. "I want to go to England for university, but my dad wants me to stay close to home. We're still arguing about it."

"Wow!" Gabriella said. "Do you mean like Oxford or Cambridge? You're so smart you could get in anywhere."

"I don't really care where," Evelyn said. "As long as it's out of this country."

"What's wrong with *this* country?" Riley asked.

Evelyn took a deep breath and let it out. "Nothing that I'm prepared to say in front of you."

"O-M-G," Riley said. (That stands for "Oh my God," Dr. Corbin.) "Just because I disagree with you doesn't make me an informant!"

"Not yet," Evelyn said.

"What?" I said. "What do you mean?" I turned to Riley. "Did you get a job? Are you going to be an informant?"

Riley frowned. "No. I'm not going to be an informant. I'm also not going to spend all my spare time alone in my bedroom, believing every conspiracy theory some dowdy loser posts online." Then she smiled at Evelyn and said, "By the way, I *love* what you've done with your hair, Evelyn. What stylist do you use? You didn't do that yourself, did you?"

It was nice of Riley to say, but honestly, Dr. Corbin, Evelyn just had her hair in a loose braid. It wasn't even a particularly good one, with plenty of curls already escaped and falling over her face. She has red hair like mine—like mine used to be, I mean—but curlier. If she spent a little time on it, it would look gorgeous, but she mostly throws it into a ponytail or a braid and forgets about it.

I touched my own head, thinking of my lost hair, and accidentally brushed one of the scabs where you cut my head open. My scabs still hurt a lot when the painkillers wear off.

Evelyn noticed me wincing. "Okay," she said. "Visit's over. Lauren's tired. Time for you guys to go."

"I'm okay," I said.

Evelyn ignored me. "Thanks for coming! Come again soon." She waved her hand at my friends like she was shooing flies out of the room.

When they were gone, Evelyn sat on the floor, leaning against my bed. Her shoulders slumped.

"I just accidentally touched my scab," I said. "I'm not tired."

"I'm tired," Evelyn said. "Tired of your friends. Sorry." She picked up Mr. Piglet, one of my old stuffed animals, and put him on her lap.

Neither of us said anything else for a few minutes. This is pretty normal. Evelyn comes into my room all the time, and lots of times we don't talk. Sometimes she brings her computer with her and does her work while I watch a video or something. This time she just hugged Mr. Piglet and sat there.

After a while I yawned.

Evelyn stood up and kissed my cheek. "Have a nap," she said. "Dr. Corbin said you'd need lots of rest for a few weeks."

"I know."

"Just remember our rule," she said.

"I remember," I said.

She left, and I fell asleep. I slept for a few hours, until some little kids playing outside woke me up. Then my mother brought me some soup, and then I felt well enough to get all this down.

I have to say, Dr. Corbin, that so far I don't think your operation has helped much. After I talked this entry into my tablet, I read it over twice, and I still don't understand lots of what Riley and Evelyn were talking about this afternoon. Did Evelyn really think that some people who disagreed with Dr. Newman got him arrested as a sex offender? If so, wouldn't that make her really mad? I don't think she was really mad today. And why did Evelyn make Riley leave right after Riley complimented her on her hair? Does that make sense to you?

I'm so sick of not understanding anybody.

My head hurts and I'm going back to sleep.

Your friend,

Lauren

JOURNAL OF
LAUREN C. FIELDING

Dear Dr. Corbin,

Nothing much to say. My head hurts, but not as much. I watched a lot of shows today, and even read a few pages from a novel we're meant to read for English class. *The Catcher in the Rye*—have you read that, Dr. Corbin? So far I hate it. It's all: blah blah blah, this person is phony, that person is phony. The author is such a complainer.

To be honest, I almost always hate novels.

At least with math you know where you stand. You learn what a right triangle is and from then on, you can always recognize a right triangle. It's not like English, where you read a short story and you don't know if the narrator is lying or telling the truth until the teacher tells you.

Anyway, sorry I don't have anything more exciting to report, Dr. Corbin.

Your friend,

Lauren

CASE NOTES OF
DR. FINLAY BRECHEL

December 4, 2031

Two days in. Given Lauren's pronounced paranoia with respect to Dr. Corbin, I've asked Dr. Corbin to avoid all contact with Lauren, at least until Lauren's mental state is more stable. Despite the privileged information that Lauren believes went online today, Dr. Corbin has continued to respect my wishes, casting further doubt (as if I needed it) on Lauren's version of events.

I've also requested and been given access to the forms Lauren signed when she committed herself to the Paxeon Clinic. As Corbin assured me, Lauren freely committed herself to the clinic. I'm guessing that, in an unusually lucid moment, Lauren realized she needed help and also realized the best place to get it was the one medical clinic in the world with expertise in her condition.

My initial theory about what's going on is this: a successful treatment of Lauren's former condition left her ill-prepared for the routine dishonesties of everyday life. I understand from Dr. Corbin that she's attempting to come up with a treatment that will roll back some of the changes in Lauren, mitigating Lauren's paranoia without risking her cognitive gains.

Personal note—I need to keep a close eye on misplaced feelings of sympathy for Lauren. That skinny teenaged girl in handcuffs and ankle cuffs has put at least two therapists in the hospital and permanently crippled one of her order-lies. Presuming the report is accurate, Eric Schafer, her former orderly, will never regain proper use of either his left leg or his right hand. (Which reminds me—I should visit Schafer to hear his version of events.)

That said, I would like very much to have more information on the background of Lauren's case. In particular, why has Dr. Corbin invested so much time and so many resources? Corbin is one of the foremost researchers at Paxeon, meaning her time is quite literally worth millions of dollars per year. What has her so interested in Lauren? And, regardless of why she's interested, why has Paxeon let her invest this kind of time in Lauren's case? Paxeon didn't become the foremost Department contractor by taking charity cases. I can't help but think I'd have more insight into Lauren's situation if I understood more about the treatment Dr. Corbin developed for her.

JOURNAL OF
LAUREN C. FIELDING

Tuesday, October 14, 2031

Dear Dr. Corbin,

Today was my first day back at school!

You should be very proud of yourself! My head hardly hurts at all now, and I think I'm getting the hang of *not* believing everything people say. Like this morning, when Evelyn and I were leaving for school, my mom asked Evelyn, "What's wrong?"

Evelyn said, "Nothing." She didn't look at my mother—just said "Nothing," and walked out the door before my mother could ask anything else. And I thought to myself, *That's not true.* That probably would have been obvious to any normal person, but before your treatment I would have shrugged and thought, *Great! Nothing's wrong with Evelyn.*

I don't know what's bothering her, but something is definitely on her mind. Today was another beautiful fall day, red and gold leaves blowing everywhere, but Evelyn frowned the whole way to school. And all she wanted to talk about was her stupid rule.

One of the things that would be great if your treatment works is that I could finally forget all about *the rules*. Did my parents tell you about them? When I was a little kid, and my parents were just figuring out that I wasn't normal, my father came up with five rules for me. The idea was that I would memorize the rules and they would compensate for how much I trusted everyone. Like Rule #1 is "Don't get in the car with anyone not on the safe list." Rule #2 is "No touches from anyone not on the safe list." Over the years we've added rules, until now there are eight of them.

I do my best to follow them, but I can't always resist. I love hugs! So I can't *always* follow Rule #2! And I just don't see the point of not giving my friends money if I have it (breaking Rule #5).

All the rules but one have come from my father. On my tenth birthday, Evelyn brought me into her room and gave me Rule #7. She had me copy the whole thing about a dozen times—by hand, on *paper*, until she was sure I had it memorized. Then she lit a fire in her trash can and burned the paper that I'd written it on. Since then we've done the same thing every year on my birthday.

It's a long rule, but I can recite it word for word without even trying: "Never repeat anything you hear someone else say about the authorities. The 'authorities' means: the government, the police, the sponsoring corporations, and most especially, the Department. Don't even repeat it to me (meaning Evelyn). Break this rule, and you will get people in trouble."

When I turned fifteen, I told Evelyn I still remembered her rule and I didn't need to write it another ten times. Evelyn grabbed my shoulders, stared into my eyes, and said, "We're going over the rule. You're my sister. I love you. I don't want anyone making you into a snitch."

Dr. Corbin, how could someone *make* you into a snitch if you didn't want to be one? But when Evelyn gets that tone in her voice, I just do what she says.

Anyway, the whole walk to school, all Evelyn wanted to talk about was her rule. What's funny is this is the one rule I've never even been tempted to break. I break pretty much every other rule at least once a month. Like the week before the operation, my special education assistant wasn't paying attention during lunch, and Jimmy Porten convinced me to eat a cockroach. (Breaking Rule #3—"Never accept anything to eat or drink from anyone not on the safe list.") But I've never—not once—broken Evelyn's rule. So I don't know why she was making such a big deal about it this morning.

Other than that, my first day back at school was fine. Everything's pretty much the same as last year. Except for the new kid, Sasha, who turns out to be in every one of my classes. I can see why Riley thinks he's cute. He has bright blue eyes and light brown hair, both of which set off what my mother would call his "peaches-and-cream" complexion—you know, rosy cheeks, good skin, etc.

After school, when Riley was driving me home, she kept asking me questions about him.

"Where's he from?"

"Um. I think I heard him say New Mexico. His father works for the Department."

Riley rolled her eyes. "We live in Bethesda, Lauren. Everyone's father works for the Department. Why does he wear glasses?"

"I don't know," I said. "Because he's nearsighted? I used to wear glasses before I got the laser surgery."

Riley shook her head impatiently. "So why doesn't he get the surgery?"

"Maybe he can't afford it," Gabriella said.

"If his parents were that poor, he wouldn't be able to afford to go to our school." Riley turned onto my street, frowning to herself. She honked and waved at Ms. Thompson, our old English teacher, who was gardening in her front yard. "And they definitely couldn't afford to live around here." Riley's eyes widened. "I bet he's working for a reality television show about high school. I heard they use cameras mounted on glasses all the time to capture point-of-view footage."

"Wow," Gabriella said. "That would be cool. Hey, Lauren, you'd be like one of the stars because you're in all his classes."

I touched my bristly scalp. "Ugh. No way. Not until my hair grows back."

No offense, Dr. Corbin, but I wish you had used more stitches to close up the scars on my head. It looks like the hair isn't going to grow back there and the scars are super-big and ugly.

"It looks great," Gabriella said.

I didn't say anything, but I'm almost positive Gabriella was just saying that to be nice. I would swear that she doesn't really think my hair looks great. I guess that's the bad part of not believing everything people tell you, right, Dr. Corbin? There are some lies it's nicer to believe. But it was still kind of Gabriella to say that, don't you think? So it still made me feel better, even though I think I'm going to wear a hat to school tomorrow. Or maybe a scarf—like Ms. Warnecke (the music teacher at my school) did when she had breast cancer and lost all her hair.

Anyway, I'm super-excited that I'm starting to be able to tell when people are lying, even if it's just white lies like that. Thanks again, Dr. Corbin!

Your friend,
Lauren

CASE NOTES OF
DR. FINLAY BRECHEL

December 4, 2031

Transcribed from interview:

Reading your journal, it sounds like you really missed your hair.

At first, yeah. I really missed my hair.

Is there a reason you haven't grown it back? By now it would easily be long enough to hide your scars.

I'm not interested in hiding anything. Plus, with no hair there's nothing for people to grab if . . . when I get into fights.

Do you anticipate getting into many more fights while you're at this facility?

Actually, I anticipate getting murdered while I'm
at this facility.

(pause)

You don't seem so funny today, Dr. Brechel, no
offense.

I noted your reaction to the drugs yesterday and
Dr. Corbin has changed them accordingly. You
understand she's just trying to stabilize your
condition.

I understand that's what you think. Why were you
asking about my hair?

I was wondering if there was someone in particular
who liked the way you looked with a shaved
head. Someone who might have changed the
way you thought about it.

(Long pause. Subject audibly sighs before asking:)

What's today?

Today is December 4. The day your—ah—
information was meant to be made public,
correct?

Yeah.

So do you remember our conversation yesterday?

I remember. I think it's a little early for me to
conclude that I'm totally wrong about Dr. Corbin.
Maybe the folks at the Department haven't
noticed my post yet. Maybe Corbin is still

hoping you can convince me to take it down.
Maybe she thinks it will be easier to call me
crazy if I'm locked up here instead of dead.

If I may, I'd like to point out that you're
transforming the facts to fit your theory.
Yesterday you suggested they'd kill you today if
you hadn't told me a password. Now you're
suggesting "they" may keep you alive indefinitely.
This is a classic strategy of a wounded
psyche, Lauren. You're forcing the facts—
whatever they are—to conform with your
version of the world.

Doesn't everyone do that?

(chuckles) Maybe. I suppose the idea here is for us
to come up with a version of the world that lets
you live more happily with other people.

Speaking of me living, has Congress voted to
extend the Emergency Act?

I believe the House of Representatives has approved
a bill, but a few senators are holding out, asking
the usual questions around government
oversight of the Department.

The usual questions. Ha. They're going to start
asking some less-usual questions when they see
the stuff I've posted online. I know—you think
this is all delusional. But they're not delusions if
I'm right.

(pause) Ahem. I don't think you answered my earlier question—was there someone in particular who liked your hair short?

(sighs) A few people, I guess.

Like who?

(long silence)

My self-defense teacher, for one. Mr. Benitez loves my hair like this. (smiles) He would give every girl in his class a crew cut if he could. Any time he sees a girl's hair getting long, he can't help himself. "What? You want to give the scumbag something to grab? Why you gotta make his life easy?"

Ah, yes, Mr. Benitez. I believe I read about him in your journal. You're quite fond of him, aren't you?

I wouldn't say that. He's a good self-defense teacher, that's all.

JOURNAL OF
LAUREN C. FIELDING

Thursday, October 16, 2031

Dr. Corbin!

I'm actually getting better at reading people! I just went to my first self-defense class since the operation, and you'll never believe what happened!

Evelyn and I have been going to self-defense classes two or three times a week since I was in fifth grade. It used to be fun. A lot of us started around then. You know, because after the Emergency, everyone's parents were like, "You have to learn to defend yourselves!" Never mind that my father can barely throw a punch himself.[4]

---

[4] The self-defense movement flourished in the U.S. for several years after the first uprising, in a kind of widespread fantasy that being a better fighter could somehow help you if there was another uprising. I think people were just desperate to believe there was *something* they could

I've hated the classes ever since I turned twelve. That was the year they made us start seriously sparring. My friends had all dropped out by then, and I would have dropped out in a second if my father had let me. I hate sparring. We all wear mitts, a helmet, and a mouth guard, but a punch in the face still hurts. A punch in the stomach really hurts. And I've always been bad at it.

It's not that I'm slower or weaker than the other girls in the class. I have no problem breaking boards—actually, I'm better than lots of the boys at that. I'm fast, too. Not to brag, but last year my teacher, Mr. Benitez, told me I'd be one of the best fighters in the class if I was just a little more aggressive. The problem is, I don't want to be more aggressive. I don't want to hurt anyone. This doesn't seem to bother any of the other kids, but I'm always worried that I might break someone's nose or something. What if their face never looks quite right afterward, and it's my fault?

I thought I wouldn't have to go back to the classes for a few more weeks—not until my head was totally healed—but today at dinner my father said, "Don't eat too much, Lauren. You're due at Benitez's in forty minutes."

"What? I can't go." I gently touched my head where you sewed me up (the wounds are still pretty itchy, by the way). "My head hasn't finished healing."

---

do. (I'd argue that it was very much the same impulse that led to the passage of the Emergency Act and the attendant restructuring of the Department, with its heightened tools of surveillance and prosecution.) In any case, the self-defense fad had run its course by 2031. When Lauren wrote this journal entry, Mr. Benitez had maybe half the number of students he'd had in the immediate aftermath of the Emergency.

"You're going." My father pointed his fork at me. "I called Dr. Corbin and she said the exercise would be good for you. You just can't spar."

I don't think I stopped smiling for the next half hour. I was almost skipping as I followed Evelyn to the car. I kept thinking: *I don't have to spar. I don't have to spar.*

Evelyn saw me smiling and laughed a little as she got in the driver's seat. "Mr. Benitez is not going to be happy when he hears you can't spar." She shook her head and imitated Mr. Benitez's bass voice. "Hey, how you gonna learn to take a punch without taking a punch?" Mr. Benitez says that at least once every class, usually when someone's crying because they got punched in the stomach. He's kind of a jerk, Mr. Benitez. Mrs. Benitez is much nicer, but she mostly works with the little kids.

The gym's a few minutes down the highway. Close enough to the District[5] that it almost feels like you're in the city, but not so close that it's actually dangerous.

We got to the gym with a few minutes to spare and changed into our practice clothes: T-shirts and sweats. Another of Mr. Benitez's favorite questions is, "What, you gonna be in a uniform

---

[5] By "District," she means the remains of what was at the time still formally called Washington, D.C. After the first uprising in 2025, the Department enclosed and monitored the hardest-hit areas of the city (while the wealthy northwest portions were incorporated as a separate municipality). By 2031, when the events in this book took place, the political organs of the U.S. government had long since been relocated to the more easily secured Virginia suburbs, while the Department and its associated contractors (like Paxeon) had mostly set up shop in Maryland suburbs like Bethesda.

when you get into a fight? Someone attacks you, you gonna say, 'Excuse me for a minute. I need to change into my karate uniform'?"

I don't know why this means we should wear sweats. I pretty much never wear sweats, so chances are pretty slim that I'd be wearing sweats if someone attacked me.

Mr. Benitez came over to us when we walked into the gym. He's a short guy, with a big stomach. He doesn't look especially strong, but I've seen him break six pieces of wood with a punch. Not a full-body punch, either. He doesn't wind up or anything. Just— pow—one punch and the wood breaks.

Benitez ran his hand over my head. For a guy who spends so much time hitting people and objects, his hands can be surprisingly gentle. "What, you imitating my hairstyle?" He's mostly bald with a little fringe of graying crew cut.

I was about to answer no, when I realized he was joking. Pretty cool, right? *I* realized he was joking. No one told me. I just figured it out myself.

I smiled. "Nah. My hair already looks better than yours."

Benitez smiled, then cocked an eyebrow. "Evi been giving you smart-ass lessons or something?"

"Or something," Evelyn said. "Hey. Lauren can't spar today. She's still recovering from the surgery."

He stepped back. "All right. You girls start warming up. Evi— when you're ready, you find yourself a partner and get to work." He glanced at me. "You, I don't know . . . start on the speed ball and move to the heavy bag when you get bored."

45

Benitez teaches a grab-bag mix of jujitsu, boxing, and dirty tricks. His assistant teachers are all men, and they all wear jock protectors. Benitez encourages us to kick them between the legs whenever we're sparring. "It's a good habit," he always says. "God forbid I get my girls in the habit of fighting fair."

I was punching the speed ball, wearing mitts and a helmet, when Devon Malachi walked in. Devon's a good guy. He graduated from our high school last year, but when he was a senior and I was a sophomore he always smiled at me when he passed me in the hallway.

"Hey Lauren," he said. "You been sick or something? I haven't seen you around here for weeks."

I nodded. "Yeah. I've been recovering from surgery."

"Cool." He feinted a punch at my face, then hesitated, his forehead wrinkled.

"What?" I said. "What's wrong?"

"I just feinted a punch and you didn't duck. You always duck."

"It was just a feint," I said.

"Yeah. But you always . . ." He frowned again, then feinted another punch at my head. This time he shifted his feet a little, and I could tell he was going to follow up with a real jab from his other hand. I ducked, and his punch went whistling over my head.

He grinned a little wildly. "Holy crap," he said. "What happened to you?" He jogged up and down a little and jabbed at my face again.

I ducked again. "Stop it, Devon!" I said. "I'm not supposed to—"

He leaned back on his right foot and I knew he was about to snap a kick toward me with his left foot.

I lunged at him, planting my foot behind his right leg, and shoved him backward. I caught him off balance and he went down hard, with me on top of him. I shoved my forearm into his throat. "I'm recovering from surgery," I hissed at him. "I'm not ready to spar yet."

Devon grinned at me. "You could have fooled me," he said. "That was awesome!" His eyes went to the fringe of stubble peeking out from under my helmet and his smile vanished. "Oh my God," he said. "It was brain surgery? I figured it was like an appendix or something. I'm so sorry." His brow wrinkled. "But still. You totally kicked my butt."

I pushed off him and got to my feet.

"Devon," Benitez called, his voice like a whip crack. Devon shot to his feet. "Whose gym is this?"

"Yours, Mr. Benitez," Devon said loudly.

"Give me a hundred push-ups," Benitez said. "Next time you come to class, you wait until I tell you what to do."

"Sorry, Mr. Benitez," Devon said. His eyes lingered on me for a few seconds before he dropped back to the mat and started doing push-ups.

The rest of the class was a little boring, honestly. I worked the heavy bag really hard, but all I could think of was the feel of Devon's throat pinned beneath my forearm. You wanna know the crazy thing, Dr. Corbin? It felt *awesome*. Like I'd been spoiling for a fight all day without realizing it.

You'll tell me when I'm okay to spar again, right, Dr. Corbin? I think I'm going to like it a lot more now.

CASE NOTES OF
DR. FINLAY BRECHEL

December 5, 2031

Transcribed from interview:

Tell me more about your fight with . . . (pause)
Devon Malachi.

It wasn't a fight, Dr. Brechel. It wasn't even a real
sparring match. Devon was just messing
around. It was no big deal.

So you say. I note that it's the first time in your
journal where you talk about enjoying violence.

I'm telling you—it wasn't violence. It was like a
two-second play fight.

Lauren, one of the reasons we're here is your
escalating tendency toward violence.

I don't have an "escalating tendency toward

violence." And if I do, it has nothing to do with why you're here. You don't really think that Dr. Corbin gives a rat's ass about any violent tendencies I have?

I do. I think Dr. Corbin cares very much about your violent tendencies.

If she cares at all, she's proud of them. She probably has a little video of me kicking that orderly's ass on her phone so she can watch it at home before she goes to sleep at night. She probably . . . (shakes her head). Shoot. Don't get me started. I think there's still an outside chance they'd let you walk away. Which you should do as soon as possible. At some point in the near future, it'll be too late.

(silence)

All right. Let me propose something to you, Lauren. You spent the first sixteen years of your life without any ability to be suspicious of others. Without any ability to read their emotions or to conceive that they might be thinking something other than what they were saying.

Dr. Corbin's treatment changed all that. And now you can't turn your suspicions off. In my eyes, your pathological paranoia is the natural outcome for a person who suddenly has to come

to grips with all the social messiness of the
world.

"Pathological paranoia"? The funny thing about
paranoia is, it depends on the truth, right? I
mean, it's only paranoid if I'm wrong.

I want you to consider the possibility that you are
*wrong. You said it yourself in one of your journal
entries—that perhaps a side effect of the therapy
was making you too paranoid. Just consider that
possibility.*

Sure. I'll consider the hell out of it. When my
guards walk me back to my room, take off my
handcuffs and ankle cuffs, and lock the door, I'll
consider it all night long.

JOURNAL OF
LAUREN C. FIELDING

Monday, October 20, 2031

Hi Dr. Corbin,

My father says you want me to come in this weekend for a checkup. It'll be great to see you again! I think you'll see that your treatment totally worked. Every day I feel like I understand other people a little bit better.

It's not as fun as I thought it would be.

I don't mean to sound ungrateful, but understanding other people is sort of terrible sometimes.

Like after English class today. I walked out of class and I happened to see Riley down the hallway talking to the new kid, Sasha. I waved at her. She smiled and waved back. Then she said something to Sasha, looked at me, and laughed.

It was between classes, so the hallway was filled with people.

It was way too noisy for me to hear what Riley said. She could have said anything. Still, I'm almost positive she was saying something unkind about me. I don't know how I know this. But even her smile was fake, with a kind of look-how-nice-I-am-smiling-at-stupid-little-Lauren feel to it.

Do normal people feel that way when they see their friends? Is this maybe a side effect of the therapy—that I might be getting too paranoid? Or is this real? How do normal people tell the difference?

Then, later, at lunch, Riley kept looking over her shoulder at Sasha, who was sitting a few tables away from us. He was hunched over his tablet computer, glasses perched on his forehead.

"He keeps looking over here, too," I told her.

"Who?"

"Sasha," I said. "Isn't that who you keep checking out?"

Gabriella and some of the other girls laughed, and Riley flushed a little. "No."

"Then who are you looking at?" I glanced over at the table where Sasha was sitting with a bunch of the non-jock guys. "Adam Dominguez?"

"I'm not looking at anyone, Lauren."

"My mistake," I said. "I just thought it was nice. You know, you checking him out, and him checking you out."

"Seriously—he was checking me out?"

I nodded. "Every few seconds." At that moment, Sasha's eyes flickered up from his screen; he noticed me watching and waved. I waved back.

"Are you . . . Don't wave at him!" It obviously took her some effort, but Riley didn't turn her head.

"Oh. Sorry. He waved at me first."

"Maybe he's checking Lauren out," Molly Singh said.

And everyone laughed. Like that was a big joke. I know I don't look so good right now, with my crew cut and scars on my head. And I wouldn't necessarily expect Sasha to be interested in me, even if I still had my hair and everything. But still, Dr. Corbin, it didn't feel good. The whole table laughing at the hilarious idea of a good-looking guy checking me out.

"What's wrong, Lauren?" Gabriella said. "Is your head hurting? It looks like you're about to cry."

My whole life, I've been an easy crier. I've cried at pretty much every movie I've ever seen, even if I've watched it like thirty times before. Even if it's not a particularly sad movie. I could never hide it if I felt like crying. I never wanted to hide it. If I felt sad I cried. I never thought twice about it.

Today, though, I didn't want to cry in front of those girls. I didn't want them to know I cared.

And you know what's weird? It was easy to fool them. I made my lips stop trembling and I forced myself to smile. "Just the sun in my eyes," I lied.

I thought they would all see right through me, but not a single person said anything more about it. Not because they were being polite, either. They believed me.

I usually get a ride home with Riley, but after school today I decided I wanted some time to think. I used to wonder what it meant when people said that. Evelyn or someone would say, "I need some time to think," and I'd wonder, "Aren't you already thinking? Isn't everybody always thinking?"

But now I get it. It really means you need time away from other people.

For a normal kid, walking to my house from the school would be no big deal. It's less than a mile and our neighborhood is totally safe. You can't even get off the highway around here if you don't have the right permit for your car. The gates won't open, and the police will pull you over if you linger in the exit lane for more than a few seconds without the right electronic tag.

Still, I'm not allowed to walk home by myself. (Rule #8 having been established two years ago when I nearly got run over by a car while I was crossing Old Georgetown Road. It wasn't that I didn't see the car—I was just sure the woman driving would stop for me. And she did . . . Just a little too late.) So I called Evelyn.

"Hey," I said. "Could I walk home with you today?"

Evelyn didn't say anything for a few seconds. Before your treatment I probably wouldn't have made anything of the silence, but today it was pretty clear. My own sister didn't want to walk home with me.

This didn't make me feel any better.

"Today is kind of a bad day, Lauren," she finally said. "Can't you get a ride with Riley?"

"I don't want to. Please, Ev."

She sighed. "Okay. I'll meet you outside the back door at three twenty."

After my last class, Ms. Gale, my special education assistant, walked me over to the back door to drop me off with Evelyn. This is basically Ms. Gale's job—walking me to the bathroom and to my classes, making sure no one takes advantage of me when no teacher is looking.

"Thanks, Ms. Gale," I said once I spotted Evelyn.

"No problem. Have a nice evening, dear." Ms. Gale quickly walked away, fishing her car keys from her purse.

"Hey," Evelyn said. She barely glanced at me, keeping her eyes on the crowd of students walking past us. "What's wrong?"

"Nothing."

Evelyn shot me an astonished look. "Oh my God. You're lying. Not very well, but still. The operation actually worked." She hugged me. "Lauren, that's amazing."

"Yay," I said, without much enthusiasm. "I thought being normal would be more fun."

"Why? What happened?"

"Nothing really. Today I realized that Riley and Gabriella don't really like me. And even you didn't want to walk home with me."

Evelyn took a deep breath and blew it out. She released me from her hug, but left one arm wrapped around my shoulders. "Welcome to the wonderful world of social awareness. Don't take it personally. Riley and Gabriella like you fine. They just don't *love* you quite as much as you thought. They're kind of fake, but they're like that with everyone, not just you. In fact, I think they're probably less fake with you than with anyone else they know."

Evelyn scanned the crowd of students passing us. "As for me, this just happens to be a bad day for you to walk home with—hey, Peter!" Evelyn spotted her friend Peter and grabbed his arm. She pulled him outside with us.

"Oh. Hey Evelyn. Hey Lauren." Peter looked at me, squinting against the fall sunshine. "I heard you were back in school." He touched his head where my head was scarred. "How you doing?"

"Okay," I said. "How about you? I heard you were abducted by Dr. Newman."

Before Peter could say anything, Evelyn quickly said, "I told you he wasn't really abducted by Dr. Newman."

"It's okay. Everyone's heard the rumors." Peter closed his eyes and pinched the bridge of his nose between his thumb and forefinger. "No one abducted me."

He certainly looked like he'd been abducted, or maybe trapped in a coal mine. Every bit of color had been bleached from his face. Except for beneath his eyes, where there were dark circles. He'd lost weight, too, since the last time I'd seen him before my operation. "I was visiting universities. Harvard. Yale. Columbia. It was great."

I didn't even think about believing him. His voice was too flat, his eyes focused far behind me.

"Lauren's walking home with us," Evelyn said brightly, maintaining a tight grip on Peter's biceps, like she was afraid he was going to run away.

"You guys shouldn't be seen with me," Peter said. "Especially not outside the school. Claudia's right."

Claudia Rich is my sister's other best friend. She and Ev and

Peter have all been good friends for years, so I have no idea why she'd be telling Evelyn not to walk home with Peter.

"I can decide that for myself," Evelyn said.

"Can she?" Peter nodded at me.

Evelyn took a deep breath before turning to me. "Lauren—do you have your headphones on you?"

"Yeah."

"Do you mind listening to music while we walk home? And walking like half a block ahead of us? Peter and I have some private stuff to talk about. I'll keep an eye on you, but I don't want you listening. Okay?"

She waited until I nodded.

"Thanks," Evelyn said. "Start walking. Remember to wait for me before you cross any of the major streets."

"I can cross a street by myself," I said.

"Most of the time," Evelyn agreed. "Most of the time you can."

I put on my headphones and started walking.

"Can you hear me?" Evelyn called after me.

I didn't exactly intend to eavesdrop on them, Dr. Corbin. I was just a little curious about what was so secret. Plus, I was . . . I am . . . so sick of people telling me what to do.

So I left my music off and pretended I didn't hear Evelyn. I walked through the parking lot, then up the road toward our subdivision, Evelyn and Peter trailing behind me.

At first I really couldn't hear their conversation, even with no music. But then Peter started talking louder and louder. We were a few blocks from the high school—just passing the middle school—when I heard Peter say, almost shouting, "You think it mattered what I said? They didn't need my denunciation. He was already screwed. But if I hadn't given them something, I would still be in there."

Evelyn said something I couldn't hear.

Peter said, "I didn't owe him anything. He ruined my stinking life. Who cares if he was right about the Emergency Act or not? Thanks to him, the Department has a file about me. One e-mail from them and I'm done. No university would take me if the Department told them not to. I'd be lucky to get a job pouring coffee."

Evelyn said something soothing, but Peter wasn't soothed.

"If you really believe the Department is going to let the Emergency Act expire in January, you're dumber than Lauren."

I turned around, forgetting I wasn't supposed to be listening. Neither of them noticed. They had stopped walking and were facing each other on the sidewalk.

"Lauren's not dumb." By now Evelyn was talking pretty loudly, too. "And getting detained by the Department doesn't make you a super-genius—it just makes you scared. All these interrogations are just the panicky last gasp of a bunch of people who know they're about to be shut down. The people on top have already moved their money out of the country. They know what's coming."

Peter's voice got quieter all of a sudden. "I was in class when Newman said all that. And look where he ended up. Even if the Department releases him tomorrow, he'll never teach again. He'll probably never work again. He'll wind up dying in some debtors' prison in the District. You want to know what's coming? A second Emergency. A third one. No one's going to dismantle the Emergency Act."

"Look," Evelyn said. "Newman got in trouble because he was talking in front of the class. It's not against the Emergency Act for me to say things to you one-on-one."

Peter shook his head and took a few steps back from Evelyn. "You know what's against the Emergency Act? Whatever the Department says is against the Emergency Act."

"I get that you're scared," Evelyn said. "You were detained for a few days and I can't imagine how terrifying that must—"

"I'm not scared!" Peter said, though he obviously was scared. Terrified, even. I'm not sure how I knew this. I think it had something to do with noticing that he was blinking a lot and that his right cheek had a little twitch. "I'm just seeing things clearly for the first time in my life. The Emergency Act started the Department, but nothing is going to stop it. Anyone who . . ."

Peter realized that I had walked back to join them and let his voice trail off. He smiled at me. A small tight smile that looked painful. "Oh. Hey Lauren. Did you hear me say . . . I'm sorry I said you were dumb, Lauren."

"It's okay," I said.

He raised his hand. "See you guys around." He quickly walked back down the hill, taking another route home, I guess. Or going back to school.

When he was half a block away, I turned to Evelyn. "Does Peter's face always get that twitch when he's scared?"

Evelyn stared after Peter. "The cheek thing? I guess. I never really thought about it."

"So how did you know he was scared?" I asked.

Evelyn hesitated. "I don't know," she said. "I just knew." She pulled my headphones off my head. "You weren't listening to music, were you?"

I shook my head.

"Remember my rule," she said. "Don't—"

"I remember your rule," I quickly interrupted. "Don't repeat it in public."

"This isn't supposed to . . . We're supposed to be able to talk to each other . . ." She started crying and half turned away from me.

I put my arms around her. Evelyn hasn't cried in front of me for as long as I can remember. She buried her face in my shoulder and made little snuffling noises. Then she took a tissue from her pocket and blew her nose. "Goddamn it," she said. "Of course I believe that the Department is crucial to keeping our society safe, but I wish I could continue to be friends with Peter, despite his occasional lapse in judgment."[6]

---

[6] This is the first place in her journal where I'm sure Lauren deliberately fabricated something, in this case to protect me—futile as *that* effort turned out to be. I suspect I actually said something like, "The Department is scared because the Emergency Act is about to expire and the Department will finally be held accountable for its crimes." Or something similarly hopeful. As though if only the Department didn't exist, there would suddenly be enough food for everyone, and the richest people in the world would peacefully hand over their wealth to be distributed to the starving refugees who were already almost everyone else.

I have to tell you, Dr. Corbin, that I wish I hadn't already told you about Evelyn's rule for me. I want you to know that Evelyn has never said anything against the Department or any sponsoring corporation. Her rule was just trying to keep me safe.

To be fair to my seventeen-year-old self, I wasn't the only one who thought getting rid of the Emergency Act would solve the world's problems. This was six years after the first uprising, remember, and the remains of the U.S. middle class were finally poking their timid heads up, like groundhogs wondering if it was safe to come out of their holes. It wasn't, of course, but at the time we were hopeful.

CASE NOTES OF
DR. FINLAY BRECHEL

December 6, 2031

Transcribed from interview:

*I've been reading the journal entries you sent to
    Dr. Corbin, and I'm wondering about the episode
    where you walked home with your sister and
    Peter Connelly. I note that, in that journal entry,
    you seem to have no problem overhearing Peter's
    side of the conversation, but you claim that you
    couldn't hear almost anything Evelyn said.*

Is that right?

*Yes. Yes, it is. Why do you think it happened that
    you heard everything Peter said, but missed
    most of Evelyn's responses?*

I guess Peter was talking louder than Evelyn.

Listen. It's fine with me if you choose to lie in our therapy sessions. I do want to ask you, though, even if you choose not to tell me: was this the first time that you falsified your journal? If so, it marks an important landmark on your journey into paranoia.

Ha. Paranoia. Every day, bad things happen to people who say the wrong thing about the Department or one of its pet corporations.

Lauren. I think this is important for you to hear: that's not true. No one has ever been arrested for stating a negative opinion of a corporation or the Department in their private conversation. Public slander is illegal, but publicly slandering an individual or corporation was illegal long before the Emergency Act was passed.

Also, you should know that psychiatric therapy is not only private, but privileged private communication. You are totally immune from prosecution for anything you say here. It's like talking to your lawyer or doctor. Our sessions here are totally confidential. As long as there's no imminent risk to U.S. citizens revealed, anything you say here is between me and you.

But you're recording our conversation, right?

(pause)

That's just for my private records and use. I have

our sessions transcribed every day and use them
to inform my treatment plan.

You have them transcribed by another person?

Computer assisted, I believe, but yes, there is a
secretary involved.

So they're not *totally* confidential, then, are they?

Would you like me to turn the recorder off?

Don't bother. I'm pretty sure there's a surveillance
camera in the heating duct up there anyway.

My point is this: I want you to notice—just notice—
that, if I'm right, within two months of your
operation, you were feeling sufficiently paranoid
to start falsifying your journal entries. Entries
that no one but your doctor was going to read.

Dr. Brechel, I never had to falsify a thing to protect
Evelyn. She never slandered the Department or
a sponsoring corporation in any way.

Okay. Just think about what I said.

You too. Think about what *I* said. It's probably too
late to run now, so you should seriously consider
taking out some life insurance. Just in case.

JOURNAL OF
LAUREN C. FIELDING

Wednesday, October 22, 2031

Dear Dr. Corbin,

How was your day? Mine was okay. Interesting. A lot of firsts today.

To begin with, I lied to Ms. Gale for the first time. I wanted to walk home by myself and, of course, Ms. Gale's job is to make sure I don't do things like that. But I didn't want to get a ride with Riley and I didn't feel like inviting myself along with Evelyn again.

It's funny. I used to feel sorry for Evelyn for only having two friends. Now I think that that's two more friends than I have. I still sit with Riley and Gabriella and the other popular girls at lunch. But now I realize I'm not really their friend. I'm more like . . . their mascot or something.

Anyway, I told Ms. Gale I was getting a ride with Riley as usual. Then I dragged my feet getting my stuff together. At 3:20—when Ms. Gale is supposed to be done with work—I was still at my locker.

She sighed, looking at her watch.

"You can go, Ms. Gale," I said. "I'm okay getting to the parking lot by myself."

"You sure, hon?" she said.

"Definitely." I gave her my best smile. "No problem."

"All right, dearie," she said.

And just like that, for the first time in my life, no one was watching out for me. It felt . . . weird. Sort of freeing, sort of lonely. I walked toward the back exit, wondering if most people feel this way all the time.

Outside it was another crisp fall day. I zipped up my jacket and shoved my hands into my pockets. I hadn't gone far, maybe a dozen steps into the parking lot, when someone called for me to wait up.

I turned and saw Jimmy Porten hurrying after me. He's a big guy, Jimmy. Plays football, though not so well that he ever gets to start.

"Hey Lauren," he said. "Are you allowed to walk home by yourself now?"

I shrugged. "Not really. Almost. I'm getting better."

"You are? That's great." He started walking next to me. "I'll walk you home."

Once we got out of the parking lot and halfway down the next block, he put his arm around me. He has a big arm and having it slung around my shoulders made it a little hard to walk. Still, it was okay until we were walking through the little wooded area behind the middle school, and he started to pull me closer and closer. His hand brushed the top part of my breast.

I stepped away from him.

"Hey," he said plaintively. "Aren't we friends?"

It's probably obvious to you that he was pretending to be sad, that we weren't really friends, that we'd probably never been friends. And it was sort of obvious to me, even at the time. It's hard to explain. I felt two opposing things at the exact same time: I felt guilty for making Jimmy sad, and I felt angry at him for lying to me. It was like my brain was simultaneously working in its old and new ways and it couldn't decide which was right.

Jimmy stepped closer to me. He looked in my eyes and said, "Lauren, do you still like hugging? I have a new kind of hug I want to show you."

And again, I *knew* two different things at once. I knew I should tell him to leave me alone. But I also knew that I really do like hugs.

So I didn't do anything. In the back of my mind I was sure *someone* would do something soon. Evelyn. Ms. Gale. Someone.

I let Jimmy lead me deeper into the trees. Once we were out of sight of the sidewalk, he sat down and pulled me down beside him.

Then he turned to me, and . . . I don't know. Something clicked in my brain. I realized that no one was going to help me and that was fine. It was better than fine. It was *great*. That's how I felt all of a sudden. Like I was on my own, and instead of being frightening, it was the best thing ever.

Once I stopped being scared, I started noticing all kinds of things. Jimmy's eyes were narrowed and his breathing had gotten faster. He was excited. Not because he liked me so much (he hardly liked me at all—that was obvious just looking at the little sneer of his upper lip), but because he thought he was going to get something from me. I guess because he thought he was going to have sex with me, or maybe feel my private parts in a way that most girls wouldn't let him.

He inched his hips closer to me and I could tell—something in his body language told me—he was about to try grabbing me. He had hardly moved, you understand, but it was clear to me he was working up his courage and was just about to push me to the ground and put himself on top of me. A split second before he moved, I felt him shift his weight.

And I moved first. By the time he reached for me, I was already dodging under his arm. I grabbed his shoulder and pushed him hard in the direction he was already moving. Once a guy the size of Jimmy Porten gets moving, it's hard for him to stop. He ended up facedown in the dirt.

I jumped up and backed away from him. I wanted to get back to the sidewalk where other people could see us. Just in case. Jimmy's a lot bigger than me.

But as soon as he got up, his face and shirt covered with dirt, I realized he wasn't dangerous.

"Why'd you do that?" he said, upper lip trembling. He wiped the dirt off his face with his T-shirt. "I thought you liked hugs."

"Not from you." I walked the rest of the way back to the sidewalk, and he followed me. A few middle school kids walked past us. "Not anymore."

He raised his hands and said, "Whatever. Skinhead freak. I was just trying to be nice. Why else would someone want to touch your fat ass?"

By the time he was half a block away, he was walking with his usual swagger.

I watched him strut off and I was overcome by an intense desire to hurt him. I wished I hadn't backed off so quickly after I'd pushed him down. Sure, he's much bigger than me, but I'm fast. And I'd been standing above him. I wished I had knelt on his neck and pounded his face into the dirt. He had a little dirt on his face, but I wanted there to be blood covering his face. I wanted his nose broken and his eyes blackened and . . .

Dr. Corbin, I can honestly tell you that in my whole life I have never wanted to hurt anyone like I wanted to hurt Jimmy at that moment. Like I still want to hurt him. Even now, sitting on my bed talking to my tablet's microphone, I'm picturing what it would have felt like to sit on his back, grab his hair with both hands, and slam his head into the dirt again and again. I'm smiling as I think about it. How creepy is that?

Anyway, I was standing there, watching him walk away, when a voice behind me made me jump. "You all right, Lauren?"

I spun around and almost kicked the new kid, Sasha, between the legs.

He raised his hands like he was scared. Before your treatment I would have thought he really was scared. Today I got that he was joking.

"Sorry to surprise you," he said. He looked past me toward where Jimmy was crossing the street a block away. "What was that about?"

"Nothing," I said.

"Okay. Um." He looked up the hill and fiddled with his glasses. "You walking this way?"

"What, did you hear how dumb I am? You looking to take advantage of the idiot girl?"

"Um . . . No." His eyes flickered past me, to where Jimmy was still visible in the distance. "Is that what just happened? Did that dick—"

"I told you. *Nothing* just happened."

"Right," he said. He walked a half dozen steps past me, then paused. "Hey. I think I live around the corner from you. Do you want to walk together?"

I stared at his face, looking for some sign of contempt, some sign that he was patronizing me. I saw nothing.

No. That's not right. I saw lots of things. His glasses were thick and they had a little console to one side, probably a computer that could route a video feed to and from the glasses' lenses, like Riley had said. He was wearing a bulky wool sweater that was unraveling a bit at the waist. One side of his lips was slightly turned up.

His lips, by the way, are very nice—not weirdly plush movie-star lips, but expressive. Kissable. Not that I've ever kissed a boy, Dr. Corbin (that being against Rule #2, of course).

Thanks to your treatment, Dr. Corbin, I could see something else, too. He was lonely. Really and deeply lonely. Even now I have no idea how I knew that. The way his eyes strayed past me. The way his hands were never still for more than a second or two.

I think that living most of my life without the normal ability to read people, I was sort of like someone with bad vision who doesn't want to wear glasses and can't afford the eye surgery. I learned to compensate a little for not having any natural ability to read people, so now—after your treatment—I notice more than most people.

Anyway. I could tell he was lonely. So I said, "Sure."

Sasha and I walked home together, neither of us talking much. I was still thinking of what had happened with Jimmy Porten and me. I have no idea why Sasha was so quiet—maybe that's just how he is. It turns out that Sasha lives about two blocks away from me in the house where my friend Mazen used to live.

So that was the exciting part of my day. To be honest with you, Dr. Corbin, if this is being normal, I think I was happier before. Not that I want to go back to how I used to be. The thought of someone like Jimmy Porten taking advantage of me . . . it's making me want to hurt him all over again.

Why is that, Dr. Corbin? Why would I rather be unhappy than stupid? Why not just take the happy life? What does it matter if other people thought I was stupid, as long as I was happy? Still. I'm telling you. If Jimmy Porten was here right now, I think I'd kill him. And thinking about that, I'm smiling again.

You'll tell me if I'm going crazy, right, Dr. Corbin?

Good night.[7]

---

[7] If I remember right, around this time my father and I were having loud shouting matches about the Department pretty much every night. I'm not sure if Lauren really didn't notice, or if she was already actively altering her journal entries to protect me. For my part, I'm embarrassed at how oblivious we all were to what was going on with Lauren. I recognized that she was changing, but I had no idea how fast. Not until it was too late.

CASE NOTES OF
DR. FINLAY BRECHEL

December 7, 2031

Transcribed from interview:

*So the episode with Jimmy Porten was your first
    violent interaction outside of your self-defense
    class, is that right?*

Violent? You keep using that word. I wish it was a
    violent interaction. I barely touched him.

You wish it had been more violent?

I wish I had stomped his face into the ground. I
    wish I had broken both his arms. Do you
    disapprove? How would you treat a guy who
    tried to force himself on a girl he thought had a
    mental disability?

This isn't about my approval or disapproval,

Lauren. I'm just trying to understand. Judging by your journal entry at the time, you didn't really hurt him at all. Is it fair to say you've become more comfortable with violence since then?

As though you don't know.

Hmm. Yes. Fair enough. You've injured at least five people since returning to this facility.

I think you're missing the point, Dr. Brechel. The thing with Jimmy wasn't important because of the violence. It was important because that's when I realized I didn't need anyone's help to take care of myself. And I liked it that way.

That's exactly the point. That, to you, taking care of yourself means hurting other people. Tell me about this medical orderly you put in the hospital. Eric Schafer. Were you taking care of yourself then, too?

That bastard is lucky I didn't kill him. I'm still not sure why I didn't. I was already in jail.

Lauren, you're not in jail. You voluntarily returned to our custody for treatment.

(snorts) Yeah. Voluntarily.

When you attacked Schafer you weren't restrained in any way. Another orderly—the only witness to the attack—says Schafer and you exchanged a few sentences, and then you attacked him. In the course of this attack, you severely fractured

Schafer's upper femur—his thigh bone. You also
broke three bones in his hand and permanently
damaged his windpipe. He may never walk
again without assistance, and he will certainly
never run. He can't talk or eat without pain.

Still? Are you sure he's still having a hard time
eating and talking?

Positive. I met with Mr. Schafer yesterday, and
talking definitely remains painful for . . . You're
smiling.

I like the thought of that bastard thinking about me
every time he talks or swallows.

What did Mr. Schafer say to you? The surveillance
camera in the hallway doesn't record audio and
the orderly who witnessed the attack was too far
away to hear your exchange.

Why didn't you ask "Mr. Schafer" when you saw
him yesterday?

I did ask him. He claims he welcomed you back,
and you attacked him with no provocation.

What, and you don't believe him? I'm touched,
Dr. Brechel.

I want to hear your side of the story.

That's nice, but what happened between Eric and
me . . . it's not really your business.

Lauren. I'm trying to help you.

Yeah, well, I helped myself, didn't I?

CASE NOTES OF
DR. FINLAY BRECHEL

December 7, 2031

Ms. Fielding's social observations are unusually acute. She often asks me a question and accurately anticipates my answer before I say anything. When I don't respond or when I attempt to dissemble (as when she asks questions about my personal life), she is uncannily good at divining my true response to any question.

Her own reactions are hard to catch, let alone interpret. I've taken a video recording of her face during our sessions, and looked at it frame by frame. Most people's faces show some involuntary movement every few seconds, but Lauren holds her face still for minutes at a time. A diagnosis of autism spectrum disorder would seem like a no-brainer if she weren't so damn empathetic she can practically read my mind.

Her previous condition also remains maddeningly hard to understand. Her medical record mentions a diagnosis of Williams syndrome, but even her earliest journal entries reveal far too much cognitive ability for any Williams case that I've ever heard of. It's as though she had a condition that impaired her ability to distrust others, without otherwise altering her cognitive function at all. The year before her operation she got almost all Bs, for God's sake—show me another example of a mental disability which allows someone to get straight Bs but doesn't permit them to walk home alone.

On a personal note: paranoia is contagious, especially if you're living at a secure Paxeon site with cameras visible everywhere but the bathroom. I know Lauren isn't well. I know she's not stable. She has consistently (and, so far, falsely) predicted her own imminent murder since the day I met her. And yet I've found myself wondering if there isn't enough truth in her story to put me in danger. Her perceptions of my reactions are so accurate it's hard to entirely discount everything else she says.

In any case, I've actually opened an account at one of the Swedish websites she told me about and I'm posting my case notes there as I take them. Not over the in-house network, of course—I'm not an idiot. I take screenshots with my phone and upload them via the cell-phone network whenever I leave the Paxeon complex. If some Department spybot stumbles on the transmission (or these notes), well, so be it—another reason to keep me alive.

Not to be ridiculous. I'm sure it will work out fine. I'll finish off the contract (just another three weeks to go), pass my notes over to Dr. Corbin, sign whatever loyalty oaths she wants, and walk out of here with enough money to pay the kids' school fees for the next five years. And Selena can go straight to hell if she thinks I'm going to pay their school fees without getting 50 percent custody.

If Lauren's expecting anything else from me, well . . . shoot . . . I've seen the way she looks at me. She's not expecting anything else.

JOURNAL OF
LAUREN C. FIELDING

Thursday, October 23, 2031

Dear Dr. Corbin,

Things just keep getting better.

That's a joke. Really, things are getting worse, even though my condition has never been "better." What exactly is "better" about being mad at everyone all the time? I still don't get why I'm not begging you to turn me back to how I used to be. But I'm not. I'm so grateful that I'm not dumb anymore. That I can see people how they really are.

It was nice talking to you this morning. Thanks for saying that I'm not going crazy and that it's normal that I would be so mad and want to hurt Jimmy Porten.

Do you ever want to hurt people? I sort of bet you do.

I was wondering if we could cancel my checkup this weekend.

Charlotte Montauk is having a party Saturday night and I don't want people to think I'm scared to go out just because Jimmy Porten has been spreading rumors about me.

My father says you really need to look me over in person to see how I'm doing, but I promise you—we don't need a checkup to know your treatment worked. I'll tell you about my day, and you'll see. At lunch, Riley and Gabriella didn't have to say a word to me before I knew there was something up. I saw the way Riley's eyes flickered over me and the way Gabriella puckered her lips when I sat down.

"What?" I said. "What's wrong?"

"Nothing. Why would there be something wrong?" Riley arched her right eyebrow. In eighth grade, Riley practiced that look in the mirror for weeks before she got it to look natural. These days she sees a beautician every week or two to get her eyebrows just the shape and color that she prefers.

I've tried as hard as I can to remember, but I really can't recall what it felt like to *not* think that Riley is super-fake.

Anyway, I could tell that she knew exactly what I meant when I said, "What?" I could even tell that she wanted to tell me.

"Just tell me," I said. "It's okay."

Gabriella reached across the table and took my hand. "We heard about what happened with Jimmy yesterday, Lauren." She glanced over my shoulder toward where Jimmy was sitting with the other jocks. "I think you should tell the principal."

"There's nothing to tell," I said. "It was no big deal."

"No big deal?" Riley said incredulously. "Forget the principal. I think you should tell the police."

"Tell them what? We were walking home and Jimmy asked if I wanted a 'special kind of hug.'" I rolled my eyes and shrugged.

Riley leaned toward me. "So you . . ."

"So I pushed him down and told him to leave me alone."

"What?" Riley was genuinely surprised. "Really?"

"What did you guys think happened?" I glanced between Riley and Gabriella.

"He's been telling people that you and he . . ." Riley let her voice taper off. "You know . . ."

"No. I really don't. Telling people what?" I eyed Jimmy across the room. One of his friends, Brent Anderson, noticed me looking and said something to Jimmy. A bunch of the guys sitting around them laughed.

Gabriella leaned across the table toward me. "He's saying that you're allowed to be with boys now and that you and he . . . um." She blushed and lowered her voice. "Had sex."

"What?!" I leaped to my feet. I'd calmed down a lot from the day before, but now I wanted to kill him again. I don't know if it's a side effect of your treatment, or if this is just how being angry feels for normal people, but being angry feels much more overwhelming now than it used to.

"Um, Lauren," Gabriella said. "If you go over there all angry, it's just going to make them believe him more."

"I don't care," I said. "I care about breaking his nose." As I said the words, though, I realized I did care what people thought. I didn't want anyone thinking I'd let Jimmy Porten touch me. I didn't want anyone thinking that I'd let an idiot like him take advantage of me.

"We'll tell people what really happened," Riley said. "Or you could go along with his story and we could get him expelled. Maybe even arrested. You can't have sex with someone with a mental disability."

"I don't have a mental disability."

Riley blushed a little. "I know you're getting better. I just meant as far as the school goes. You could get him in big trouble."

I knew Riley and Gabriella were trying to help me, but I wasn't—I couldn't—let Jimmy just sit at his lunch table, smirking, talking trash about me. I stalked over to his table, taking deep breaths and trying not to look as furious as I felt. "Hey, Jimmy!" I said, putting as much of my old perkiness into my voice as possible.

"Oh. Hi Lauren." Jimmy half turned and smiled like he was just noticing me. I felt a tiny bit better when I saw how nervous he was. His eyes were noticeably wider than usual and he was breathing fast, too.

"So," I said. "What have you been telling people happened between us yesterday?"

Jimmy hesitated and he flushed a little. He kept smiling, though. "Nothing," he said. "I just told them that your—um—condition is much better and we had a nice walk home yesterday."

His friends laughed and one of them, Robert Wu, muttered something about how it sounded like "a real nice walk." Another of his friends, Sean Wilton, was staring at my chest like it was a billboard.

"Great. So . . . you're *not* telling them that I had sex with you, right?" I said.

Sean Wilton burst out with a surprised laugh, then covered his mouth like he was coughing.

"Of course not," Jimmy said. "What happened between us is private."

The whole table of guys was smiling. And I realized that Gabriella and Riley had been right. It was a mistake to walk over here. Nothing I said was going to convince any of these guys— they all wanted to believe Jimmy.

"Oh, shoot. I had no idea it was private," someone behind me said. I hadn't noticed the new kid—Sasha—sitting at the next table over. He swiveled around, straddling his chair and looking up at Jimmy. He took a long sip of his soda before talking. "Because I figured it was like a public performance when I saw you try to grope Lauren and she shoved you into the dirt."

"I didn't try to grope—Lauren didn't shove me—" Jimmy narrowed his eyes. "Whatever. You weren't there. You don't know what you're talking about."

Sasha nodded thoughtfully. "I guess I was a little way off. I might have misunderstood. Were you deliberately kissing the ground? And maybe . . . was Lauren just giving you an encouraging pat on your back as you prepared yourself to make out with the"—he chuckled a little—"dirt?"

Jimmy got out of his chair and grabbed Sasha by the front of his shirt. "You weren't there, asswipe. You don't have any idea what happened."

Sasha didn't resist, letting Jimmy pull him off the chair where he'd been sitting. He held up his hands like he was surrendering. "Hey. I'm not judging. I'm sure you're a kind and"—he started laughing again and he couldn't quite finish his sentence—"a gentle . . . a kind and gentle . . . lover . . . of the dirt."

By the time he finished, all of Jimmy's friends were laughing, too. Jimmy was beet red. He let go of Sasha's shirt, and Sasha sat heavily on the cafeteria's tile floor, still laughing.

"What's going on here, kids?" My special aide, Ms. Gale, had belatedly realized something was happening and roused herself from chatting with the other teachers on lunch duty. Behind her I saw Evelyn walking toward us, flanked as usual by Peter and Claudia. I hadn't noticed Riley and Gabriella walking over, but they were standing around me, too.

Jimmy held up his hands. "Nothing," he said. "We were just joking around."

"Yeah." Sasha climbed to his feet, still smiling. "Jimmy was being really funny. I mean, this guy takes loving the earth to a whole new level."

Jimmy glowered at him, but Sasha just grinned. He nodded to me, or maybe to Riley, who was standing just behind me, and turned back to his lunch.

Evelyn pulled me away from the little crowd that had gathered. "What was all that about?" she said.

"Jimmy was telling some stories about me. Not true stories."

"Like what?"

I shifted a little uncomfortably. "About him having sex with me."

Evelyn spun toward Jimmy. "What? I'm going to break his—"

Before she could take a step, I grabbed her arm. To my surprise, Peter grabbed her other arm.

"Don't make trouble," he said. "The administration is really nervous these days and I'm sure they have their eyes on you."

Peter's face was even paler than when we'd walked home on Monday. His eyes were still bloodshot, like he hadn't slept for days.

"It's fine," I said. "It's done. No one believes him now anyway."

Evelyn glanced back at Jimmy. He was staring at the table, hunched over his lunch.

"It's fine?" Evelyn repeated.

"Yeah," I said. "I heard he was lying about me and—"

"Wait." Evelyn's forehead wrinkled. "Why would he even be telling stories about you? Everyone knows you're not allowed out by yourself."

"I walked home alone yesterday, and I happened to see Jimmy—"

"You walked home alone? Lauren, that's not safe for you."

I glanced around to make sure none of my friends were in earshot. "I didn't want a ride from Riley and . . ." I looked at Peter. "I figured you had enough on your mind."

Evelyn flushed a little. "You can always walk home with me."

"She's better off walking home by herself," Claudia said to Evelyn. "As long as you're still walking home with Peter, better she keeps her distance."

"That's not why you walked home by yourself, is it?" Evelyn asked me.

I shook my head.

"It doesn't make it not true," Claudia said, not looking at Peter. "Being seen with Peter outside of school is just stupid."

"He didn't do anything wrong," Evelyn hissed. "And it's not illegal to hang out with someone who was detained and released."

Claudia sighed. "I don't like it any better than you, Ev."

"You sure seem to," Peter said.

"Oh, I'm sorry," Claudia snapped, finally turning to look at Peter. "Aren't I sympathetic enough that you got detained for posting Newman's lectures on your webfeed? How could you be so stupid?"

I started easing away, figuring they had forgotten about me.

"Lauren," Evelyn said sharply. "I'll meet you at the back entrance at 3:20." She spun and walked away, Peter and Claudia trailing after her like bickering goslings after the mother goose.

"What if I don't want to walk home with you?" I muttered, but not loud enough for Evelyn to hear.

The truth is, when I walked out the back exit this afternoon, it was nice to find Evelyn waiting for me. She was standing by herself, to one side of the main flow of students, frowning and staring at the soggy leaves that had collected in the gutter at the edge of the parking lot.

"It's a beautiful day," I said. I stuffed my jacket into my backpack, enjoying the feel of the sunshine on my bare arms.

"Yeah." She started walking, and I followed.

"Peter's not coming?"

"No." She frowned and looked so sad, I almost cried. "It's not a good idea right now. Not with Dad's contract with the Department up for review, and with the Emergency Act pretty surely going to be reauthorized what with the thing in China and . . ." Evelyn shook her head as she remembered who she was talking to. "Anyway. He's not coming."

We walked down the hill, over the little bridge behind the middle school. A dog barked in the distance. "What thing in China?" I asked.

Evelyn gave me a long look. "You heard about that?"

"You just mentioned it."

"Shoot. I didn't mean to . . . It's nothing for you to worry about."

"What happened?"

Evelyn thought for a few seconds.

"Ev, if you don't tell me, I'll just look it up when we get home."

"It's not that. I don't know how to explain it to you."

"You don't have to dumb it down—" I said.

"I didn't mean dumb it down—"

"And I won't say anything inappropriate where anyone else can hear. Just tell me."

She looked at me thoughtfully. "Okay. Yesterday, the premier of China got caught in a brothel and said all sorts of things to the press about how corrupt everyone in his government is, along with details about payoffs and payouts and *everything*. So now he's been deposed and put in jail and there's this big conflict in the Chinese government about who gets to take over."

"What does that have to do with Dad's job?"

She shook her head. "Some aide to the premier claimed the U.S. drugged his boss. You know, to sow dissent, so the Chinese government would be too distracted to mess with U.S. interests. There's been a lot of talk lately about how China is outpacing the U.S. in its foreign influence, so this whole thing is pretty much a dream come true for the U.S.

"The Department is denying having anything to do with it, of course, but only in the kind of way that makes you think this was all them. It's made a bunch of congresspeople say they're definitely going to vote to extend the Emergency Act, which, you know, would mean the Department would go on being the Department. Which means Dad will still be bidding on contracts for them for the foreseeable future.

"Besides . . . you know Dad. He gets scared of his own shadow when he's between contracts."

I hadn't known that at all, but I resolved to pay more attention to that kind of stuff now that my brain is working right. "The funny thing," Evelyn said, "is that the whole thing in China probably had nothing to do with the Department. Probably the premier of China just got caught in a brothel and figured if he was going down he might as well take a few of his cronies with him." Evelyn glanced behind us and frowned. "Can you walk faster?"

I followed Evelyn's gaze and saw Sasha walking up the hill

after us. I waved at him. "Why?" I said. "I know that guy. He's really nice."

"I know him, too," Evelyn said. She grabbed my wrist and pulled me after her. "He works for the Department. Look at those glasses: they're obviously for recording."

"Riley and Gabriella said that was for a TV show."

"As if," Evelyn said. "A single-camera reality show? That dude works for the Department."

"So does Dad," I said, feeling defensive. I liked Sasha. Not just because he was good-looking, either. "So do half the grownups we know."

Evelyn looked at me pityingly. It felt very familiar, suddenly. Evelyn looking at me pityingly and explaining something. The story of my life until a few weeks ago. "Lauren," she said. "Dad does policy work for the Department. This guy is an *informant*."

I pulled my hand from her grip and turned to take a good look at Sasha striding after us.

Evelyn shook her head with disgust. "Look at him, with the video console right out where anyone can see it. He's a professional informant for the Department and he's not even trying to hide it."

"Why would he hide it? That's *why* the Department sent an informant to our school. They want us to know. Knowing there's an informant around makes people less likely to say stuff they're not supposed to. Just like having a police car on the side of the road makes people stop speeding. Which is the whole point, right?"

Evelyn thought about it. "Who told you that?"

"No one. It's obvious. They send one agent to the school and everyone's too scared to do . . . whatever it is they're worried we're going to do. Much cheaper than arresting a bunch of people."[8]

Evelyn gave me another long look. "And you figured that out yourself?"

"I guess the treatment's working. Anyway—" I glanced behind us. Sasha had long legs and he was catching up to us without seeming to hurry. "I don't care if he works for the Department. I like him. He made Jimmy look like an idiot for lying about me."

"Lauren," Evelyn said. "We both know that no one is a bigger supporter of the Department than me,[9] but it's not safe for you to hang around him. Just in case you say something that could be taken the wrong way."

Another few seconds and Sasha was right behind us.

Evelyn stopped walking, obviously waiting for him to pass us. Instead, he stopped, too. "Hey Lauren," he said.

"Hey." I returned his smile.

"I'm Sasha." He held out his hand to Evelyn.

Evelyn looked at his hand without taking it. "I know who you are."

He shrugged and put his hand back in his pocket.

---

[8] In fact, this was explicit Department policy at the time, as detailed most recently in the paper "Not-Too-Secret Service: The Department's Use of Undercover Agents in the Inter-uprising Period" (Christensen et al., *Annals of American History* 209 (2040): 437–459).

[9] It probably goes without saying that I never said that, or anything close to that.

"She thinks you work for the Department," I said.

"Lauren!"

"It's okay," Sasha told me. He told Evelyn, "Obviously you're right."

"You're not even going to deny it?" Evelyn said.

"Definitely not. If I lied, you might get angry enough to say something stupid about the Department in front of my video feed, which might eventually get watched by someone who cares about that kind of thing. I don't want you getting in trouble. And anyway, what's the point of denying it? Why else would I be wearing these glasses?" He touched the recording apparatus next to his right lens, and the briefest hint of anger flickered across his face, vanishing so fast I wasn't positive I had seen it.

He took a deep breath, his face a picture of pained sincerity. "Listen. I know the glasses are creepy. The thought of some Department bureaucrat watching you walk home . . . I get it. But I know those bureaucrats and they're just people. They're doing what they think is right to protect their country. They're not monsters. No one wants you to get in trouble just because your politics are a little wrongheaded."

"*My* politics are wrongheaded?" Evelyn flushed, outraged.

"No offense."

"I'm pretty sure he's telling the truth," I put in before Evelyn could respond. "About not wanting to get you in trouble, I mean."

"How would you know?" Sasha said.

Evelyn opened her mouth and quickly closed it, obviously wondering the same thing but not wanting to agree with Sasha.

"Not sure," I said. "I'm still figuring out this whole 'working brain' thing."

"Why don't you think about it while we walk?" Evelyn said. She took my arm again. "Bye-bye," she told Sasha.

"Um. You go on," I said. "I want to talk to Sasha."

"I'm not leaving you alone with him."

"I'll be okay," I said. "Please. I'll be there in a second. I just want to ask him something private."

Evelyn stood there for a few moments.

"Please," I said again. "Do you trust me?"

This is a reference to the old Disney version of *Aladdin*.[10] It used to be a kind of joke between Ev and me, back when I trusted *everyone*. Funny how long ago that seems now, even though it's only been, what? Not quite two months since the treatment. Just about a month since I've been back at home.

"Of course I trust you," Evelyn said.

"Then go. I'll see you at home." I tugged my arm free and gave Evelyn a gentle nudge to start her going. I waited for a few minutes as she walked away.

Sasha whistled tunelessly, hands in his pockets. "Nice day," he said.

"Yep," I responded. I wasn't sure if Evelyn was out of earshot yet.

Below us, the wooded parks around the schools were a blaze of autumn colors in the sun. There was a distant smudge of gray

---

[10] 1992. Walt Disney Feature Animation.

where the smoke rose from the District, but around us it was all sun and blue skies and brightly colored leaves.

"You know," Sasha said, once Evelyn was out of earshot, "your sister completely underestimates you."

"Yeah, well. I've changed pretty quickly." Evelyn turned to look at us, and I waved at her. "Smile," I said quietly to Sasha. "Pretend I just told you Riley thinks you're cute."

Sasha didn't hesitate. He gave me a wide smile and laughed, just the right hint of pleased incredulity in his voice.

Evelyn looked confused, but she kept walking. I was almost positive she was already out of earshot, but I still counted to twenty before speaking, just to be sure.

I looked intently at Sasha. "Why are you following me?"

"What? I'm not . . ." Sasha stopped himself, no longer smiling. He catches on quick, Sasha. He'd been about to lie, but then, guessing that I would know if he lied, he settled for evading the question. "It's just that I live near your house."

"You're following me. You obviously saw exactly what happened between me and Jimmy yesterday. You couldn't have seen that without following us into the woods."

Like I said, he's fast. It took him a split second to come up with an explanation. "Well, sure, I followed you into the woods. I happened to be walking home behind you yesterday, and when I saw you walk into the trees with Jimmy, I trailed along. I didn't want him to . . . you know . . . take advantage." He hesitated. "When I saw you didn't need help, I came out the other side of the trees and made it look like I just happened upon you. I thought you might be embarrassed otherwise."

"Sure," I said. "Which brings me back to my original question—why are you following me?"

Sasha's lips twitched, like he was fighting a smile. Like I said yesterday, he has very attractive lips. For lots of girls, his half smile would be just about as distracting as he thinks it is. I was not distracted. I waited.

"You heard your sister," he finally said. "It's my job to follow people."

"The Department assigned you to follow me?"

He hesitated, then nodded.

"Why?"

"I have no idea. I follow who they tell me to." His eyes were wide and sincere behind his thick glasses, but I wasn't sure he was telling the truth. His eyes are pretty distracting, too, honestly. They're a deep blue the color of the summer sky ten minutes before full darkness. "Someone with a lot of pull must be interested in you."

"Shouldn't you be better at keeping it secret?" I had a sudden urge to grab his glasses and throw them as far as I could.

"Probably," he said. "To be fair, you weren't supposed to be like some super-perceptive girl who would see through my well-told lies. They told me you were . . . *innocent*." His face went still when he said "innocent." I couldn't read it at all. It was the first time that had happened to me for days. Funny to think that I used to walk around and every face was like that.

"Anyway," he said quickly, like maybe he had let something slip that he shouldn't have. "You wouldn't have been on to me so fast if I hadn't had the ridiculous idea that you might have needed help dealing with a guy twice your size."

"I appreciate that. But I still want to know why you're following me."

"I'll tell you if I find out."

I rolled my eyes. "Sure you will. Listen, you can't let Evelyn know that you're following me. She's a little protective."

"Wait, are you telling *me*, a highly trained agent for the Department, to keep my mission secret?"

"Well. You do seem to have a little problem with keeping things to yourself."

He laughed, seeming honestly amused. Then, glancing behind me, where a few other kids were walking home, he said, "I should get going or people will think you're an informant. See ya." He waved his hand and started walking.

I walked after him, lost in thought. Why would a government agent care if other people thought I was an informant? And why would the Department be having me followed? Dr. Corbin, excuse me for asking, but did you ask the Department to have me followed? Why would you want me followed? If I come in for more tests this weekend will you tell me?

Evelyn was waiting in front of our house when I got home. "What did you want to talk to him about?"

"Oh nothing," I said, smiling a little shyly. I obviously couldn't let Evelyn know Sasha was following me. She'd lose her temper, confront him, and say something that would get her in trouble. "Just . . . Riley thinks he's cute and I wanted to see if he was into her."

Some of the worry left Evelyn's face and she just looked disgusted. "Are you serious? He's an agent for the Department, for God's sake. And anyway, what is Riley, twelve?"

Weird to think that a couple weeks ago, I would have thought Evelyn was seriously asking me if Riley was twelve. Even now I had to fight back the temptation to answer her with *No, she's sixteen!*

Evelyn went on. "If she's so curious, let her ask for herself."

"It's not like she asked me to ask him. I just wanted to know." I started walking up the stairs to our front door.

"So. Was he interested?"

I looked over my shoulder at her and pretended to be confused. "Are you asking me if Sasha 'likes' Riley? Aren't you too mature to ask that kind of question?"

Evelyn followed me. "Oh come on. What did he say?"

"No, no. Don't let me bring you down to my level. I'm sure you have more important things to worry about than . . . Hey! Stop!" Evelyn was tickling me under my armpits. "Stop it! Okay. Yes. He said if he wasn't here on official business, he'd definitely be interested."

"Oh my God," Evelyn said. " '*If he wasn't here on official business*' . . . What a total prick. What a prick of a prick. Like he's here on some noble mission instead of to narc on anyone he can. I support the Department's mission, but I do find these tactics objectionable."[11]

---

[11] Again, Lauren protecting me. I'm not sure why she didn't just delete this whole exchange. It's almost like she was taunting Dr. Corbin, like, "I know you're reading this, and I want you to know this isn't an accurate account."

I laughed, relieved that she wasn't planning to do more than hate him.

Walking up to my room, I put my hand in my sweater pocket and found a little slip of paper. It said: *The tree house, tonight, 10:30—S.*

The crazy thing is—I'm totally going.

Your slightly
insane friend,
Lauren

CASE NOTES OF
DR. FINLAY BRECHEL

December 8, 2031

Transcribed from interview:

*When did you start falsifying your journal to
Dr. Corbin?*

Shoot. I don't know. A few weeks after the
operation. At first, it was just a little bit here, a
little bit there. Mostly around things that Evelyn
said or didn't say. Editing any statements that
might have given someone the impression that
Evelyn was in any way opposed to the
Department's methods. Which, of course, would
be totally wrong—Evelyn's a big supporter of
the Department. Like any right-thinking person.
(laughs)

Still, once I realized that anything I sent Dr. Corbin might well get back to the Department . . .

I understand. You were worried about the close association between Paxeon and the Department.

Ha. The "close association." Nice one, Dr. Brechel. I don't think they drugged me today, but I still think you're pretty funny.

And did you falsify more as time went on?

Of course I did. The more aware I got that everyone was not my friend, the more I falsified. And once I guessed that the Department was having me followed on behalf of Dr. Corbin, well, shoot . . .

Mind you, as of four days ago, you can find something pretty close to my honest journal entries online. I'm not suggesting they'd be the healthiest thing in the world for *you* to read, but then again, by now it's probably too late for you to back out anyway. If you're curious, just do an Internet search for "Lauren Fielding" or "the Innocence Treatment."[12]

You've mentioned this before, but just to be clear—you kept two versions of your journal?

(laughs) It does sound kind of crazy when you put

---

[12] To be clear—all journal entries included in this book are rendered in their online version, in part because I don't have access to the (presumably more falsified) versions that Lauren sent to Dr. Corbin.

it like that, but who else was I going to talk
to? I didn't want to get anyone I trusted
in trouble. (long pause) Speaking of which—is
there any chance I could get a notebook and
a pen? I'd like to start keeping a journal in
here, too.

I don't see why not. Let me make a note. I'll have
them bring you a tablet—

Not a tablet. Not a computer of any kind. Just a
paper notebook and a pen, please. I don't want
anything with a network connection.

Ah . . . It'll have to be a blunt pencil, given your
history of attacking orderlies. And of course, if
you attack anyone—

I think we can be pretty sure the next violent
episode that I'm involved in will be decisively
directed at me. Pencil or no pencil. What did you
say today's date was?

December 8.

I genuinely don't get why I'm still alive. Even if I
gave you my password now, even if they took
my post down, it's not like it would help them.
Too many people would have seen it.

Lauren. I promise you. That's not why they hired
me. No one has mentioned any secret passwords
or online material that we have to take down. I

know you're good at telling when people are
lying to you, so tell me. Am I lying?
(long silence)
You believe you've been hired to help me. That
doesn't make it true.

JOURNAL OF
LAUREN C. FIELDING

Monday, October 27, 2031

Hi Dr. Corbin,

Nice seeing you this weekend!

Okay. That's a lie. Honestly, it sucked seeing you.

You know why it sucked? Because you were lying to me. Not just with your words ("No, Lauren, I have no idea why the Department would have someone following you. Are you sure about that? . . ."), but with your expression, with that kindly little smile. It's like a plastic Halloween mask. I don't know how I missed it, even at the height of my naïveté. It freaks me out, honestly, how totally fake you are.

You were happy to see me, that much was true. But you weren't happy the way a normal person is happy to see someone. More like . . . it reminded me of this show I saw a few years ago about people trying to catch a monarch butterfly during what everyone knew was the monarchs' last migration before they went extinct. I remember the look on this one guy's face when he caught his butterfly. You were happy like that.

Anyway, I don't think you have any doubt that your operation worked, so I don't understand why you're so eager to get me back into your lab. Do you mean to change me back to how I used to be? Is that it? I don't get why you'd bother. In fact, I don't get why you'd bother fixing me in the first place. I've done some research in the last few days and it makes no sense. As best I understand it, Paxeon is more or less the research brain of the Department. So why would you want to help me?

I'm *almost* tempted to believe your explanation about how "a bit of paranoia is completely natural given your completely innocent state beforehand." It *is* weird that pretty much everyone I know (except Evelyn) has turned out to be a liar. Even my father, for God's sake. Maybe I'm not super-perceptive—maybe I'm wrong. Maybe Gabriella really does love the way my head looks all stubbly and studded with scars. Maybe you really do want to help me out of the goodness of your heart. And maybe the moon really is made of delicious green cheese. None of that seems too likely, though.

I asked my father yesterday, when he was driving me home from your office, "Dad, how did you find Dr. Corbin in the first place?"

If I was someone else I probably wouldn't have noticed how my question startled him—he didn't say anything and his face stayed perfectly still. But his knuckles whitened as he squeezed the steering wheel and his hands jerked right just a smidgen.

"Actually, she contacted me," he said. "I always hoped you could be a little more . . . independent, and she said she might be able to help you."

"Oh." I watched the countryside go by for a little. It's a nice drive out to Paxeon headquarters—it's located due north from our house, so you don't see all the burnt-out buildings that you get near the District, nor the gray military bunkers you get in Virginia. It's mostly farms and forests and the occasional small town. "So Corbin contacted you out of the blue?"

He hesitated. "Yeah." I read the lie in half a dozen little things. He stopped glancing at me every few seconds, instead keeping his eyes trained on the highway, even though there was hardly anyone else on the road, and anyway, the car pretty much drives itself on the interstate. He started tapping the steering wheel with his right forefinger.

I pressed him. "Didn't it strike you as weird? That a Paxeon scientist would offer to help me? Don't they mostly do work for the Department?"

His forehead wrinkled. "Well," he said reasonably, "Paxeon is a huge research institution. I think Dr. Corbin took an interest in your case for the pure science of it. Plus maybe as a way of giving back."

"So you never met Dr. Corbin before last year?"

"No." Lie number two. Which, okay, was pretty much the same as lie number one.

"Dad . . . Please. Tell me the truth."

He shot me a quick glance. I've noticed this: Most people (not you, Dr. Corbin, but most people) don't like lying. Not about important things.

"Okay," he said, abruptly relaxing. "Sorry. It just . . . It takes some getting used to. The new Lauren."

"You're used to being able to lie to me."

He snorted a little. "Only to protect you, sweetheart. The truth can be uncomfortable."

"So make me uncomfortable."

"Your mother and I first met Dr. Corbin about eighteen years ago. Years before she started working for Paxeon. She actually helped your mother and I get pregnant with both you and Ev."

And this, finally, was the truth. Harder to believe than the lie.

"What?" I said. "You needed help? But Dr. Corbin isn't a . . . a fertility doctor."

"She's a geneticist." He fidgeted with the car's audio console. "Dr. Corbin was doing some consulting with fertility clinics back then. She pioneered the DNA-manipulation techniques that allowed your mother and me to conceive. I think she always felt a little guilty that you came out"—he reached over and gently touched my scarred, crew-cut head—"a little different. So it wasn't totally out of nowhere that she wanted to help."

"What? Why didn't you tell me all this before?"

He sighed. "When you've been keeping a secret for sixteen years, it's hard to stop. We never wanted you to be any more self-conscious about being different than you already were."

"You didn't even tell Ev?"

He shook his head. "She had such a heavy load to carry anyway."[13]

By which he meant the heavy load of being my sister. Fair enough, I guess.

His explanation for why you helped me would have made sense if I hadn't just met with you and seen the way you were looking at me.

I spent the rest of the ride home thinking of those old fairy tales where the witch or evil fairy or whoever helps someone, and then comes back years later to take their baby. Like Rapunzel, where the pregnant mother wants lettuce from the witch's yard, and the witch gives it to her, but then—surprise! she tells her she'll be back for the baby.

Point is—I don't think it was an accident how I came out. Were you trying something with Evelyn, too, and it didn't work? Or was she the control and I the experiment? Is that why you messed me

---

[13] My father filled me in a few days after Lauren got the story out of him. I'm not sure of the precise date, but it had to have been right around then because I remember not believing him, assuming it was just one more tactic in his ongoing campaign to make me hate the Department and Paxeon a little less.

I blush to remember the way I spoke to my father back then, like he was nothing but a Department collaborator, cravenly terrified that I—his noble, truth-speaking daughter—might harm his prospects at work. In retrospect, of course, he was just being a concerned parent, trying to keep me out of trouble. And given the stigma around "designer babies" (genetically engineered humans being even more taboo then than they are now), of course he wouldn't have wanted to tell us any sooner than he had to.

up? Just to see what would happen and then to see if you could fix me? Did you learn something useful at least?

The real bitch of this is I can't ask *you* these questions. I can't even tell you I know you're lying. The second you know I'm onto you, I'm pretty sure you'll figure out a way to force me back to your facility. I have no idea why, but I could see it on your face this morning—there's no way you're letting me go.

So I have to let you think that I'm still a naïve little girl, while I use whatever freedom I have left to figure out what's going on. Along those lines, I'm going to delete this entry and write a whole new one to send to you.[14] One with lots of exclamation marks!

Your friend

(but not really),

Lauren

---

[14] Clearly Lauren decided not to delete this entry, instead saving it for future dissemination. The following entry (which I presume is the one she sent to Dr. Corbin in place of this one) appears to be more or less truthful, if occasionally insincere.

JOURNAL OF
LAUREN C. FIELDING

Tuesday, October 28, 2031

Hi Dr. Corbin!

Nice to see you over the weekend. You asked me to think about this question: is it easier to tell when some people are lying than others? The answer is definitely yes.

My old friends—Riley, Gabriella, and all the others—they're totally easy to read. Like this morning, Riley came by my locker and gave me a big hug and said, "Lauren, you look so gorgeous today! Your hair is really starting to come back in!"

Everything about her said she was lying. Her voice—a little higher pitched than usual. Her smile—bigger than her real smile. Even her eyes, staring just above my shoulders instead of looking at my face when she talked.

I think she really was trying to be nice, so maybe it shouldn't bother me. Thing is, Dr. Corbin, it does. I don't like people lying to me, even if it's just to be nice.

Funny thing is, Sasha told me he liked my hair today, too, and I totally believed it when he said it. Sasha is much harder to read than Gabriella or Riley. Maybe it's his glasses making it harder to see his expression, but he almost always seems sincere when he talks to me. I guess this might just mean he's a better liar than anyone else I know. It should make hanging out with him more stressful. With Riley and Gabriella, at least I know where I stand. With Sasha, everything he says could be a lie.

And yet. He's super good company. We've started walking home together pretty much every day.

Today I picked him up at his locker on my way out of school. "What's with the scarf?" he said as we walked out the back door. It was a warm afternoon, almost summer-warm, but I had a big silk scarf wrapped around my head.

"Spare people the sight of my bad hair day slash month," I said. "Not to mention the sight of me picking at my scabs." (Which are still super-itchy, Dr. Corbin!)

"I think your hair looks great," he said casually.

"Yeah? What about my scars? You like the way they look?"

"On you? Sure. You want to see some *ugly* scars?" He lifted his shirt and showed me a scar going from under his belly button to just under his right nipple. It was raised and pink, about as wide as a finger, and looked like no doctor had even tried to stitch the skin together afterward.

"What's that from?" I asked.

He shrugged. "The exciting life of an undercover agent."

That rang false. I don't know where his scar came from, but I'm almost sure it had nothing to do with working for the Department.

You want to know what's funny? Catching Sasha in the occasional lie makes me trust him more. It gives me more faith that the rest of the time, when I think he's being sincere, he really is.

It's hard to tell: am I actually getting good at telling the difference between truth and lies, or is it all just in my head? What do you think?

Your friend,

Lauren

CASE NOTES OF
DR. FINLAY BRECHEL

December 9, 2031

Transcribed from interview:

*Reading your entries, it sounds like you became
good friends with Sasha Adams despite the fact
that you believed he was a Departmental agent
specifically assigned to spy on you.*

Yeah, well. Unlike everyone else, he didn't miss the
old me. The kind, stupid, pretty me.

*Interesting how you refer to the old you in the
third person, as though you were a different
person.*

C'mon, Dr. Brechel. Of course I was a different
person. Corbin killed the old me as surely as if
she lopped off her head.

About Sasha Adams: is it fair to say you found him attractive?

(laughter) It's fair to say most inanimate objects would find Sasha attractive. Not just because he's so good-looking—although he is *very* good-looking—but because he has that way of concentrating on you. Most guys, they look at you, and you sense them checking out your boobs or thinking about a movie they watched the day before or whatever. Maybe just zoning out and thinking about nothing at all. Sasha had this vibe, that when he looked at you, he really looked at you.

I wasn't the only one who noticed. Two months after coming to our school, he was one of the most popular kids in my grade. The fact that everyone thought he worked for the Department just seemed to add to his mystique. The drug dealers and the political types stayed away from him, but what did anyone else care? At least you could be pretty sure his recordings wouldn't end up posted to the Internet.

Every time we walked home together, three or four kids would stop to offer him a ride. Girls, guys, gay, straight . . . everyone wanted to be his friend.

How often did the two of you walk home together?

Pretty much every day. He was going to follow me anyway, right? And he was a pleasure to hang out with. He has a great sense of humor. Plus, hanging out with him made the Department seem less scary and more like the old—what do you call it? Like in the old movies? The FBI. Keeping people safe.

I've read your journal entries, Lauren. The ones you sent to Dr. Corbin, I mean. Not the ones you've apparently posted online. But I'm still not sure I understand why you were sneaking out of your house to meet Sasha in your old friend's tree house at night.

What's your guess, Dr. B.? Why do you think a sixteen-year-old girl and an extremely good-looking seventeen-year-old boy might sneak off at night to meet in a secluded tree house?

You weren't really . . .

Go on. You can say it.

You're saying you were romantically involved with him.

I don't know if I'd say "romantically" involved. Neither of us is the most romantic of sorts.

What word would you choose?

Sexual. Physical.

You were sexually involved with the agent assigned to follow you?

You don't have to sound so shocked. I used to be
  prettier.

*I'm not . . . I'm not shocked that he would choose to
  be with you. On the contrary, I'm not sure I
  understand your decision to be with him. Did
  he . . . coerce you in some way?*

What? No! Never. Not in any way. Listen—out of
  everything that's happened in the last three
  months, hooking up with Sasha is the one part I
  don't regret. Not even a little. So he works for
  the Department—so what?

I hope he's okay, that's all. Me posting my real
  journal entries may not have been the best thing
  in the world for his career.

JOURNAL OF
LAUREN C. FIELDING

Thursday, October 30, 2031

Dear Dr. Corbin,

Got your phone message today. (And yesterday. And the day before yesterday. Are you getting a little impatient with me, Dr. Corbin?)

It sounds like you really want to hear about when I snuck out to meet Sasha in the tree house. I wish I had never told you about the note Sasha slipped into my pocket. At the time I figured you'd hear about it via his report to the Department, but now I'm not so sure.

So yeah—last Thursday, when I got home, I found a slip of paper in my jacket pocket. A scrap torn from a lined notebook. *The tree house, tonight, 10:30—S.* A little presumptuous, if you ask me. Dude didn't even bother with a question mark.

He must have had the note written out already and shoved it into my pocket while we were talking, making sure his glasses were pointing somewhere else. Seemed a little melodramatic at the time. Because, like I said, at that point I assumed he was telling the Department everything anyway. Truth is—that still makes more sense than believing that there's a real emotional connection between me and Sasha.

But I guess I'm still a little bit naïve, because before sending this journal entry to you, I have every intention of taking out every part of my encounter with Sasha except for the kissing. And maybe a little touching . . . just to distract you from wondering what we talked about.

Speaking of my journal entries, I'm typing this on an old laptop that I dug out of the attic. I tore out the network card, so I'm pretty sure there's no way anyone could read this without physically having the computer in front of them. You'd be kicking yourself if you realized just how good I am at hiding things, right, Dr. Corbin? You did too good a job of fixing me.

Or . . . shoot. Here's a thought: Maybe you wouldn't be kicking yourself at all. Maybe you'd be totally proud of yourself if you knew. Maybe that was the whole point—to make someone who was really good at detecting bullshit, and at dealing it out themselves. Maybe I came out *exactly* the way you intended. Let's file that disturbing little thought away for later . . .

Anyway. The note said, *The tree house, tonight, 10:30.* As it happened, I knew the tree house he meant. Sasha's living in my friend Mazen's old house. When we were kids, Mazen's father built him this huge tree house in their backyard. All the kids in the neighborhood used to hang out there. It's the biggest tree house I've ever seen, built between two trees, a sugar maple and a cypress.

My parents are early-to-bed, early-to-rise types, so by 10 p.m. the only light in the house was in Evelyn's room. I tiptoed down the stairs, carrying my sneakers in my hands, and slipped out the front door.

I won't lie to you, Dr. Corbin. (Okay, I will lie to you, and gladly, but I'm not lying right now.) Even as I walked out the door, I was asking myself: What are you doing, Lauren? Sneaking out to meet a guy you know works for the Department? Seriously? Aren't you supposed to be smart now?

I didn't have a good answer then, and I don't have a good answer now. I can tell you it wasn't my old naïveté. Maybe the operation really has made me kind of crazy. You know, like a weird mix of paranoid and overconfident. After years of being so dependent on others, being self-sufficient is a little overwhelming. Like, *I can walk to school by myself now, so now I can do* anything*!* Sounds stupid, I know, but what can I tell you? That night it felt awesome.

The whole thing. Sneaking out of the house to meet a guy. A guy I knew I shouldn't like, but who I kind of did, anyway. Just being outside after dark on my own. You have no idea what that's like— when you're sixteen years old and you've *never* been outside after dark on your own. It was a cold night, the kind of fall night where you can't believe you were wearing a short-sleeved shirt a few hours before. I was wearing my thickest fleece, but I was still cold.

I jogged to Sasha's house, partially to warm up, but mostly

because it was fun to run through the suburban darkness on my own. I felt like a ninja, slinking through the neighborhood seeing everyone, no one seeing me. I caught little glimpses through our neighbors' windows, the Jensens watching television, Ms. Amos shuffling around the living room in her pajamas.

The porch light was on at Sasha's house, illuminating a recycling bin full of crushed soda cans and empty macaroni and cheese boxes. The tree house was a dark mass in the yard beyond. I didn't see Sasha anywhere, so I went ahead and climbed up on my own.

It's been years since I climbed a tree, and that felt awesome, too. Pulling myself up the maple tree as fast as I could. Climbing more by feel than by sight in the darkness. Mazen's father had hammered a few additional handholds onto the tree's trunk, but I didn't trust them after so many years. Anyway, I didn't need them.

Once I climbed through the tree house's platform, I could see a bit better. There was a half-moon overhead, and I guess I'd adjusted to the darkness.

"Hey," Sasha said. I made out his eyes first, gleaming in the dark. Then the slim length of his body. He was lying on his side, long legs stretched out to one side of the entrance, head supported on his hand. As I watched, he sat up and turned to face me, the moonlight through the tree branches streaking his hair silver and black. "I wasn't sure you would come."

"Me neither." I glanced around the tree house. "Where are your glasses?"

"In the house. I'm not recording. I wanted a private conversation with you."

"Right." I sat down a few feet from him, trying to get a good look at his face. It was a lot harder to tell if he was lying without being able to see him clearly. "That's why you wanted us to meet here?"

He smiled and his teeth glinted in the moonlight. "Yeah. Directional mikes need line of sight, which is almost impossible through the trees. Even a satellite listening device would have a hard time fixing on us in the darkness."

"Jeez," I said. "If only the Department had an informant here to just tell them what we say." I paused and nudged Sasha with the tip of my sneaker. "Oh, wait . . ."

He laughed softly. "This isn't for the Department. Though, I gotta tell you—people like your sister just don't get it . . . The only reason they have the freedom to hate the Department is because of the Department. Her life would be so much worse if the Department wasn't around to protect her. To protect all of this." He gestured around us.

"The sky?" I said. "You think the Department protects the sky? Or wait, did you mean the tree? Does the Department protect trees?"

"I'm just saying that most people in the world would give their right arm to live in the United States under the protection of the Department, instead of under the heel of some—"

"You and Evelyn can have a heart-to-heart about that someday. Except you can't, because I don't want you going anywhere near her. Is that why you asked me here, to tell me how great the Department is?" I wondered again why I had bothered coming. Just because he was good-looking? Was I that stupid?

119

"No. Like I said, I wanted a private conversation with you."

"Why?"

He abruptly stopped smiling. "Honestly, I'm curious. I've never been asked to follow someone like you before."

"What do you mean, 'someone like me'? Who does the Department usually have you following?"

"Some druggie. I go to high schools, hang out with the druggies until I get a line on the dealer. That kind of thing." He yawned. "It's okay. The worst is the conversation. No one is more boring to talk to than a seventeen-year-old doing acid."

I hesitated. His tone had become a bit too smooth. "You're lying. What do they really have you doing?"

He cursed under his breath. "Shoot. That human-polygraph thing you do is so annoying. No offense."

"Tell me the truth or I'm leaving right now."

Sasha nodded but he didn't say anything. Not immediately. Instead he stared into the darkness, maybe wondering how much of a lie he could get away with.

I waited, too, enjoying the piney smell of the cypress tree and thinking of the bit in *Aladdin* when Princess Jasmine demands, "Tell me the truth, Aladdin!" I hoped Sasha would tell me the truth. I didn't feel like leaving.

Finally Sasha sighed. His eyes flicked back to me. "You really want to know?"

"Yep."

"The Department generally has me befriend people so I can gather evidence against their parents."

"You bastard." I couldn't help myself. "If I see you so much as looking at Evelyn or my parents—"

"Hey!" he hissed. "You asked. And I was telling the truth when I said that this thing with you is something new. I'm just supposed to follow you. That's all. They would have told me if I was meant to be gathering evidence about Evelyn or your parents, and they haven't." He grimaced. "Though, if I were you, I'd do my best to keep Evelyn away from that dude Connelly. If ever there was a guy who's begging to roll over on his friends—"

"Say it again," I said, inching closer to him so I could get a better view of his face. Our legs almost—but not quite—touching. "Put your face in the moonlight where I can see it, and promise me you are not gathering evidence against my sister or my parents."

He tilted his face toward me so the moonlight fell full on it, turning his face silver and his eyes dark. I think I've mentioned how good-looking he is. Being out at night was delicious enough, but the thrill of danger and, okay, the thrill of being near a very good-looking guy who I sort of wanted to kill. Those lips in the moonlight. Almost—but not quite—smiling. It was all a little overwhelming. I almost, but not quite, forgot to pay attention when he spoke.

"I promise you, I'm not gathering evidence against Evelyn or your parents." He met my eyes and grinned. "I come to you in peace."

I was inches away from him by then. So close I swear I could feel the heat of him radiating through the cool night air. And that's when I kissed him.

He froze for a moment, still leaning back to keep his face in the moonlight. His lips warm and still beneath mine. Then he turned to face me more fully, his arms coming around me.

"Wait, wait," he said a few minutes later. "Just to be clear. You know that I'm following you for the Department, right?"

"I didn't forget." I pulled him back to me.

Neither of us said anything for a while. We did various things that should have made us colder, what with exposing skin and so on. Speaking for myself, I didn't notice the chill.

Eventually, though, I realized the moon was in a different place than it had been when I arrived. I reluctantly rolled away from Sasha and sat up. "For the record," I said. "That doesn't mean I trust you. I just felt like kissing you."

He sat up, too. "For the record, I—um—I didn't ask you here because I wanted to get together with you."

I ran my hands over my stupid crew cut, suddenly feeling self-conscious. "Right. Well. Thanks for clearing that up."

He frowned and reached for my hand. I pulled it away. "Whoa," he said. "That came out wrong. I didn't mean I didn't want to . . . I totally wanted . . . I just didn't think you'd be interested."

I didn't look at his face, not wanting to see that he was lying. "Uh-huh. And now you'll tell me again how much you like my hair."

"Okay. Slow down. We both know I'm not telling you everything. But listen . . . look at me again. Come on."

I turned to him and found him putting his face into the moonlight again. It was darker now, though, and harder to make out his expression. I put out my hand and touched his face, laying my palm across his cheek. His cheek was cold with the night air and rough with stubble.

"I think your hair looks great," he said, his face still and his voice sincere. As far as I could tell, he was being totally honest. Either that or he's a much better liar than anyone else I've encountered since your operation. "Not just your hair. I'm totally into your whole package." He turned his face, bringing his lips to my palm, and kissed my hand. "The hair, the face, the dark humor, the thinly restrained violence, the cynicism shading toward out-and-out paranoia. I like it all."

"You make it sound really appealing."

"Like calls out to like," he said. He took my hand off his face and held it between his hands.

We were both silent for a few minutes. I'm still not sure if I was staring into his eyes romantically or searching his face for some giveaway tell. Maybe both.

"So if that's not why you invited me here tonight, tell me again. Why *did* you invite me?" I finally said. "Just because you were curious about why you were following me?"

"Look. Everyone knows the Emergency Act expires in a little over two months. Even if it's extended, I'm getting too old to work the school scene. If I lose my job, the Department will make damn sure I'm on the first flight back to the Ukrainian refugee camp where they found me."

"Ukrainian refugee camp?"

"You heard me. I lose this job, and I'm back in a camp where

I have no friends and where an American accent is like a sign on my chest saying 'Please murder me.' " Beneath Sasha's glibness, I heard real fear. "One way or the other, I need a new job soon. That's why I wanted to talk to you privately. Someone very powerful is interested in you and I want to know why."

"That makes two of us. What's your best guess?"

He shook his head, half shrugged. "Something to do with the way you used to be. Or maybe with the treatment that fixed you. I got assigned to follow you just after your treatment—that can't be a coincidence."

"Who assigned you to follow me?" I asked. "Didn't they tell you anything about what you were looking for?"

He shook his head. "It doesn't work like that. I don't think even my handler knows why I'm following you. He just got the word and passed it on. 'Follow Lauren Fielding. Befriend if possible.' " He paused like he was unsure about continuing. " 'Protect,' " he finished.

"That's why you followed me into the woods with Jimmy."

He frowned a little uncomfortably. "I'd like to think I would have followed you anyway, but yeah."

I studied his face as he stared at the thick foliage surrounding us. I was sure he wasn't telling me the whole truth, but I couldn't pinpoint the specific lie. Sasha is so coiled in on himself that it's hard for me to get a good read on him. Except when he talks about finding me attractive. That I believe 100 percent. Am I an idiot or what?

"So. You're just following orders, huh?" I said.

He half smiled. "Well, I did arrange an illicit meeting with the person I'm meant to be following. That wasn't exactly an order. Actually, if this whole thing"—he waved his arm at the tree house and me—"got back to my supervisor, I'd be lucky to avoid an immediate suspension."

"Uh-huh," I said. I tucked my shirt back into my pants and zipped my fleece up. "Let's assume you're telling the truth. You really wanna know why you're following me?"

"Yeah." He pulled his own sweatshirt back on, looking intrigued.

"Why don't we find out together? Are you any good with computers?"

"Pretty good. I've gone through a bunch of the Department's computer trainings and taught myself a bit more on my own. I'm not saying I'm the world's best—"

"You know your way around the Department's databases, right?" I've started interrupting people a lot since your treatment, Dr. Corbin. I have no patience for people finishing sentences when I already know how they're going to end.

He nodded again, looking wary. "I guess. Why do—"

"What if I get you to a computer with a direct connection to the Department's network? Could you find the files having to do with me?"

A mix of emotions passed over his face. "You're not serious."

I gave him my best smile. "I thought you could be my date to Riley's Halloween party. Someone as high up in the Department as Riley's father must have a secure connection between his home computer and the Department's servers."

He stared at me. "Is this a super-deadpan joke? You can't seriously . . . Are you really asking *me* to help you break into the Department's system?"

"It's no more illegal for you than for me," I said.

He shook his head a little—not like he was saying no, but like he was trying to clear his vision. "Even if Riley's father has a remote connection to the Department servers, it would be triple-factor protected. You'd need to know his password, have his security fob, and like borrow his eyeballs to get access."

I raised my eyebrows. "That sounds awfully complicated. I think I'll just let him log in for me."

"Why would he do that?"

"Come and see. I'm doing it anyway," I said, realizing as I said it that I was telling the truth. "After sixteen years of not knowing what's going on, I've had enough. You want to get something on your higher-ups so you keep your job? Come and help me. You know I'm not going to rat you out."

"But you don't know that I won't rat you out," he said.

"I'll take my chances. Apparently you're really into my whole package."

He barked a quick, surprised laugh. "More so every minute."

I'd feel worse about asking for Sasha's help if I hadn't seen your face last weekend, Dr. Corbin. If he rats me out, I'm no worse off— you're not going to let me walk away, anyway. The only chance I have of staying free (and with my brain in more or less working order) is if I learn *why* you're so interested.

Neither of us said anything for a few moments. I shivered a little and wrapped my fleece around myself tighter. "Hey. If you're from a Ukrainian refugee camp, why don't you have an accent?"

Seeing me shiver, he put his arm around me. I froze for a moment, then let him pull me toward him. "The Department has found that if they take kids before age eleven or twelve, they can teach them to speak with no accent. Ukrainian refugees are especially handy because we can pass as Caucasian Americans, but can be deported with no fuss. And there are plenty of us. I don't even know where they found me—one of the camps in Romania? Belarus? The Department has a slogan: 'Forget the past—be the future you want.'" Something in his tone caught my attention.

I turned to face him. "Are you lying again? That came out pretty fast."

"I'm not lying," he said. "But I have practiced that story. It's what one of my teachers called a 'sympathetic backstory.' Reveal selective snippets that make people feel bad for you. The idea being they're more likely to open up afterward." He eyed me and snorted. "I'm sure you'd prefer the 'brutal-truth backstory.'"

"You have a 'brutal-truth' backstory?"

"Sure," he said, staring straight up at the silhouetted leaves above us. "Different technique. I tell you how I testified against the father of my best friend in middle school. I describe the look on the poor kid's face as his father got sentenced to three years of Departmental detention, and as my friend realized it was his fault for telling me about his father taking him to antigovernment rallies.

"The idea is, if you tell people nasty stuff about yourself, they'll think, 'Shoot, if he's telling me such horrible, revealing things, obviously I can trust him with my secrets.'"

"Does that work?"

"You tell me. This is the first time I've tried it. Do you trust me more now?"

"Are you going to help me next week or not?"

"Help you steal data from my employer's computer system?" He tapped his fingers on his cheekbone, still staring up at the darkness. "Betray one of the world's most powerful organizations?" He took a deep breath and blew it out, shaking his head. "Pffft. I'd have to be crazy to think that's not a great idea."

He took my hand. "I presume you don't want to tell me how we're going to do it?"

"I think we should take it slow," I said. "I'll tell you next Saturday."

He laughed. "So, um. You want to fool around some more instead?"

"Actually. It's been fun, but I gotta go." I slipped off the platform, swung down on the nearest branch, and dropped a few feet to the ground, leaving Sasha invisible above me, shrouded by the bulk of the tree house and the surrounding foliage. I had to fight against the desire to immediately climb back into the tree house and tackle him. Stupid hormones.

Just between me and me: I have no idea why I didn't climb back up there. Or why I left in the first place. I had nowhere to go. I could have stayed there all night as long as I was home by, say, 5 a.m., when my dad wakes up.

I think maybe I left because I didn't want Sasha to think my body was like a reward for saying he'd help me. Or maybe because I didn't want the physical stuff with him getting in the way of my brain working right. Or maybe it was none of that. Maybe it was just because that's the fun of having a working brain. Getting to decide. Yes. No. Sometimes. Not all the time.

I'm sorry I can't send this to you, Dr. Corbin, but I have a feeling you'll be reading it someday. I have a feeling anyone who wants to will be reading this someday, posted on some website out of the Department's reach.

If and when you do find yourself reading this, Dr. Corbin, I want to say, I'm pretty sure you're getting Sasha's reports. I'm pretty sure you're the one who had the Department assign an agent to follow me in the first place. I want to tell you: you're not fooling me. Sasha's not fooling me either. If he helps me get access to my files, I'm sure he won't just be doing it because of how much he likes me. I kissed him tonight because I wanted to. I hope he doesn't tell you about our conversation tonight. I hope he doesn't turn me in for trying to break into the Department's system. But if he does, I won't be surprised. Just disappointed.

Your friend

(but not really),

Lauren

CASE NOTES OF
DR. FINLAY BRECHEL

December 10, 2031

Transcribed from interview:

Lauren, I'm here to help you. You know that, right?

You think you are. That's almost the same thing.

*I appreciate your trust, Lauren, and I'm going to
ask—*

It's not trust. I can see your face. I *know* you think
you're here to help me. It so happens that that's
not actually why you're here, but that's not your
fault. You genuinely don't know the real reason
we're talking.

*Ah. So what do you see as the "real" reason we're
talking?*

I honestly have no clue. At first I thought it was to

keep my real journals from being posted on the Web. But now . . . I don't know. They're still injecting me or spraying me with stuff most every morning—maybe Corbin is using you to measure the effects of whatever they're shooting into me. I suppose it would be hard for her to tell that I was stupid again if I wasn't talking to you.

But don't you see? That's exactly why I'm here, and that's not a . . . a sinister motive. Dr. Corbin is trying to stabilize your condition somewhere between the dysfunctional naïveté you grew up with and your current paranoia. These sessions are helping her to tell what's working.

Dr. Brechel, come on. We both know I'm not paranoid. I'm clear-eyed. The Department has almost unlimited power. Until the Emergency Act expires, they can detain whoever they want, for as long as they want. That's not a paranoid statement, that's just the truth. Dr. Corbin isn't a philanthropist. She works for a company that makes money from conflict, that supplies weapons and propaganda—mostly to the Department, but also to paying customers all over the world. That's not paranoia, either, that's just the truth.

(silence)

It scares you when I say that, doesn't it?

You can say whatever you want in these sessions. It doesn't scare—

I think it does. Your knuckles whitened a little where you're holding the pen. You're not terrified, and you're used to hiding your reactions, but that doesn't mean they aren't there. When I kept talking, your gaze flickered to the microphone, probably as you wondered if you're supposed to report such inflammatory language to the Department when Paxeon is already getting a recording of these interviews. Then you looked back at my face and relaxed a little. My guess is that you decided it couldn't hurt to include an additional note about my comments, just to cover your butt.

Lauren, of course I can't help having a reaction to such—ah—incendiary comments, but it doesn't mean you need to restrain yourself.

Ah. You're right about that. (smiles at camera) You hear that, Dr. Corbin? I have no intention of restraining myself. Now or ever. Dr. Brechel, don't you wonder why Sasha was following me?

I presume Dr. Corbin was concerned about you.

(laughs) Right. Just a concerned doctor, doing what any good doctor would do: ensure that a

highly trained, very expensive government
agent is assigned to follow her patient around.
For weeks. Do you have any idea how much that
must have cost the Department?

Seriously, Dr. Brechel. You must be wondering why
Sasha was following me, assuming, I guess, that
you believe he really existed and isn't just a
figment of my sick little brain. I was wondering
that, too. Until I got access to the Department's
database. Then I—

*Lauren. I'm not going to sugarcoat it. I believe your
condition is getting worse. Now in addition to
paranoia, you're manifesting delusions of
grandeur.*

Ha. Smart man. Makes you a little nervous when I
start telling you secrets, doesn't it? You want
me to stop talking? Just stop asking questions.
You don't have to accuse me of "delusions of
grandeur." That's kind of rude.

*Lauren, I'm not accusing . . . I'm diagnosing.
There's no way that you actually hacked into the
most secure computer system in the world. Your
treatment didn't suddenly make you a
computing genius.*

Have you still not downloaded the journal entries I
posted online? Do you think that's going to
protect you, Dr. Brechel? You've already heard

too much to just walk away. You may as well
satisfy your curiosity.

But yeah, of course I didn't "hack" into anything.
This isn't one of those movies from the '20s
where some brave hacker saves the day. Sasha
and I did it together, obviously, and there was
no hacking involved.

The Department's agent helped you break into the
Department?

We didn't "break in" to anywhere. Download the
damn journal, Dr. Brechel. It's too late to run.
You may as well know what you're neck-deep in.

JOURNAL OF
LAUREN C. FIELDING

Saturday, November 1, 2031

Dear Dr. Corbin,

Every time I write "Dear Dr. Corbin," it seems a little more ridiculous, especially now when (a) you're obviously not "dear" to me at all and (b) there's no way I'm sending this to you, you evil little two-faced, hate-mongering, life-ruining witch. I hope someone shoves a wad of hundred-dollar bills down your throat and kills you with it.

No offense.

It's after 1 a.m. and I've been lying awake staring at the screen of the old laptop I dug out of my parents' attic. Reading and re-reading the files you've been keeping on me since before I was born. Watching the video clips the Department has stuck in my file. You'd think that watching them once would be enough, but I keep finding myself opening them again.

I don't know what I thought I'd find in my file. I thought . . . I *hoped* it would be something cool at least . . . something like . . . you'd deliberately created me as the perfect killing machine. That would suck, too—don't get me wrong. To realize that my life before the operation had no purpose but to pop me out cold-blooded and clear-eyed . . . That would totally suck, but at least it would have been satisfying to be so badass.

Of course that would make no sense. No way there's a high-enough profit margin in a human weapon. You could only sell me once, after all, and sixteen years is an awful lot of time to take on a single item. Plus the Department has plenty of human—and nonhuman—weapons already. So I should have known better.

But the truth . . . You didn't design me to be a weapon so much as a . . . a production mechanism. That never would have occurred to me. A normal childhood stolen just so Paxeon could add another product to its inventory.

More and more, I'm thinking other people might be interested in what you did to me. I was already thinking about posting my journal entries, but after what I found out tonight, I'm thinking lots of people might read them. So I should probably start from the beginning of the night.

Tonight was Riley's Halloween party. Riley's birthday is the day before Halloween, so she's been throwing Halloween parties as long as I've known her. When we were kids it used to be she'd have a few girls over and we'd watch a not-so-scary movie in her home

136

theater and eat pizza and chocolate. Riley's dad is high enough in the Department that even in the middle of the Emergency they had reliable power and (even more amazing to my nine-year-old brain) more chocolate than you could possibly eat. This was at a time when everyone else I knew was more or less living on soy product and vitamin drink.

Around seventh grade, Riley started inviting boys to her parties, too, and soon thereafter having live music and DJs. This year was going to be the most elaborate party yet. Riley had lined up two live bands and three DJs—there'd be different themes in different rooms and half a dozen movie stars showing up. A ton of security.

I dressed up as an eight ball. I wanted an excuse to wear all black, not to mention to shave my head—my hair was starting to look a little shaggy.

It would have been nice if I could have driven myself, but the Department of Motor Vehicles still thinks I have a disability, so I had to arrange for Sasha to pick me up. Which at least was better than asking Ev for a ride and having to deal with her being at the party (which she would hate), not to mention ultimately having to ditch her when Sasha and I slipped off to access the Department's database (which she would hate even more).

I was waiting in our living room when Sasha pulled up in an old beater of a car. I ran out of the house, hoping to avoid introducing Sasha to my parents. Sasha walked around the car and opened the passenger door. He was dressed in a Hogwarts robe and a wizard's hat, a little lightning scar drawn on his forehead. Very retro.

"Nice costume," he said to me.

"Thanks. You too." I stepped into the car and pulled the door closed. Too late.

"Lauren!" My mother rushed out of the house, hastily pulling her phone's headset from her ears.

I got out of the car.

"What's going on?" she demanded, regarding Sasha suspiciously. "Who's this?"

"Hello!" Sasha put out his hand. "I'm Sasha Adams. Nice to meet you."

"Angela Fielding," my mother said, taking his hand. "Where do you two think you're going?"

"Riley's party," I said. "I told you this morning."

"I thought Evelyn was driving you."

"Nope."

"I offered to drive Lauren," Sasha said. He was standing straighter than usual, his eyes wide and sincere behind his thick lenses. I realized he had actually shaved for the party—it was the first time I'd seen him without even a shadow on his upper lip. I wondered what his face would feel like when it was this smooth. What his lips would feel like without any stubble surrounding them.

My mother looked from me to Sasha. She obviously had no clue what to do. To be fair, for most of my life, it really wasn't safe for me to go out with anyone she didn't know very well.

"Lauren," my mother said. "You're only allowed to go out with people on the safe list."

I shook my head. "I know that used to be the rule, but that doesn't make sense anymore. And it's only to Riley's house."

"Don't worry, Mrs. Fielding," Sasha said heartily. "I promise I'll drive straight to Riley's party and then straight back here afterward."

"Right," my mother said, seizing on the idea. "You won't go anywhere else on the way home, you got it?"

"Absolutely, ma'am."

(Yes. He called my mother "ma'am." Apparently it's true about undercover agents for the Department having no shame.)

"We'll be following the GPS in Lauren's phone," my mother said, with all the belated sternness she could muster. "If it goes anywhere but Riley's house, we'll call the police."

"We'll certainly keep that in mind, ma'am."

I kissed my mom's cheek before she could say anything else and got back into the car.

"Wait!" Evelyn jogged down the front walkway in her bare feet. Shoot. This was exactly what I'd wanted to avoid.

"Maybe next time tell your family *before* I get here," Sasha said thoughtfully, leaning back a bit on the hood of his car.

"Shut up, please," I said, watching Evelyn's flushed approach. I got back out of the car.

"Where are you taking my sister?" she asked, glaring at Sasha.

I answered before Sasha could speak. "Sasha's taking me to Riley's party."

"What, like, as a date?"

"Yeah," I said, at exactly the same moment that Sasha said, "No."

We exchanged glances.

"Not a *date* date," I said.

"Technically, it's a date," Sasha said. "But not really."

My mother looked confused and Evelyn looked suspicious. I started giggling. Turns out being nervous still does that to me.

I explained, "Sasha's not invited, so he can only come as my date."

"But really, we're just friends," Sasha said soberly. Which made me giggle even more. Whatever Sasha and I are, it's not "just friends." Every time I see Sasha, I'm torn by the urge to punch him and the desire to . . . do other things with him. I'm almost positive that's not what you're supposed to feel about your friends.

Evelyn put her hand on my shoulder. "Lauren. Did you ask Riley about bringing a Departmental agent to her party?"

"Are you joking?" Sasha asked. "Mr. Halston is the Assistant Undersecretary for Civil Affairs. I'm sure there will be tons of Department security personnel at his mansion this evening—"

"And I'm sure Riley will be delighted to see Sasha," I interrupted. For the first time it struck me that Riley might even be jealous that Sasha was coming with me.

Sasha wasn't done. "And you know what those security personnel will be doing? They're going to be keeping the party safe. That's what the Department does—it keeps people safe. Even if—"

"We should really go," I interrupted, once again wondering how an alleged undercover agent could have such a hard time keeping his mouth shut. "Can you please shut up and get in the car, Sasha?" Sasha started walking around the car.

Too late. "It keeps people safe?" Evelyn said. "Does it keep the hundreds of thousands of—"

"Evelyn," my mother said warningly.

"—incarcerated—"

I put my arms around Evelyn and thrust my cheek in front of her lips, muffling the rest of her words. I whispered to her, "Trust me. I have a plan." Behind me, I heard the car door open and shut as Sasha got into the driver's seat.

"I trust you less every time I see you with this scumbag—"

"Great!" I shouted over Ev's voice. "Have a great night!" I climbed back into the car (for the third time) and shut the door.

I waved at my mother and Evelyn as Sasha pulled away from the curb.

"Your sister's a real spitfire," Sasha said mildly.

"What part of 'shut up' didn't you understand?" I said. "Don't talk to my sister. Don't look at my sister. Definitely don't lecture my sister."

"Sorry," Sasha said, seeming genuinely apologetic. "Really. There's just something about how much she hates me . . . It bugs me. Next time I see her, my lips are sealed. I promise."

I didn't say anything for a few seconds. Sasha's car smelled powerfully of the vegetable oil it ran on. Like slightly burned French fries, with a rubbery overtone from the duct tape that had been used to repair the upholstery.

"Sorry about the smell," Sasha said. "All part of the glamorous life of an undercover agent. I put a fresh coat of duct tape on the seat in honor of our date. Which—um—may or may not actually be a date."

I snorted. "Hey. Are you planning on wearing your glasses all night?"

"Of course," he said as he turned onto Bradley Boulevard. "Why wouldn't I?"

Because we're breaking into the Department's computer system. I stared out the window, wondering if I was crazy to be looking forward to the evening as much as I was.

"Will you check the car door pocket for my wand?" Sasha asked. "I can't show up without a wand."

I glanced into the car door. "Nope. Just a few pieces of paper."

"Can you check beneath the paper?" He turned left, heading for the fortified entrance to the highway.

"There's no room for a wand in the—"

"Just check, will you?" Sasha asked. Something in his voice caught my attention. "Those pockets are bigger than they look."

I plucked the piece of paper from the pocket and unfolded it.

Don't talk about tonight's fun while I'm wearing the glasses. I can't get rid of them too early, or my handler will know something's up.

"I need the wand," Sasha continued. "Can't be Harry Potter without the wand, right? Hey, did you ever read the Harry Potter comics?"

"Uh. No. Not the books either. Fiction never made much sense to me. The whole true/not true thing, you know?" I carefully folded Sasha's note and put it in my pocket. "So you're a big Harry Potter fan?"

Sasha shrugged. "Sort of. The Department is always pushing

media toward us. You know, movies we should watch, books we should read, so we blend in better. The funny thing is, their recommendations are generally decades out of date. My handler is always bugging me to watch some crappy movie from 2018."

Sasha glanced over at me, then back at the road. "Could you check the glove compartment for my wand? I'm almost positive I had it when I walked out of the house."

I opened the glove compartment and found the wand. To one side there was an old-fashioned SD nano drive, the kind I vaguely remember my father playing movies off when I was little. It had a small green sticky note on it saying *Take me!* I put the wand on the seat between us and slipped the nano drive into my pocket. "Found it," I said.

"Great." Sasha approached the interstate entrance, and the gate automatically opened. "Personally, as far as Harry Potter goes, I liked the comics better than the books. Maybe just because they were easier for me, what with the whole English-as-a-second-language thing. You ever read *any* comics?"

"Not really. No."

I tapped my index finger on the nano drive in my pocket. If Sasha wanted to betray me, it could have been as easy as that. Put some forbidden material on the nano drive and arrange for it to be found in my pocket. Just having a storage device without a network connection was suspicious enough. *(What were you trying to hide, Ms. Fielding? What didn't you want the Department to know?)* But for whatever reason—instinct, vanity, whatever—I didn't think that was his plan.

Sasha kept prattling about his favorite comics as we drove through Bethesda. His tone was light, but the expression on his face was serious, even grim.

I was feeling pretty grim myself. After saying goodbye to Evelyn and my mother, it had occurred to me that my plan to get into the Department's computer system didn't just put me at risk, it put my whole family at risk. It's funny. I keep thinking I'm done being naïve, and then I stumble over one more blind spot in my judgment.

We drove through Bethesda, toward the Quarter—what used to be the northwest corner of Washington, D.C.

We drove through the gun emplacements at the highway exit and found ourselves in a world of big trees and huge mansions, periodic guardhouses blazing with light despite the energy restrictions.

"Wow," Sasha said as we drove through the Quarter. "I didn't think even the top dogs at the Department got paid *this* well. And why does Riley go to high school with us if she lives down here?"

"She used to live right by me," I said. "All through elementary school. But after the Emergency, her family got really rich." I hesitated, vaguely remembering my parents talking a lot about it. Their voices raised. "Her dad bought a lot of property in the Quarter right after the Emergency. It was supercheap at the time. You know, because the Quarter was still part of the city and people were freaked out by what was going on downtown. The suicide bombs, the food riots, and so on.

"Then, when the government separated the Quarter from the rest of the city, and it turned out the Quarter was still the place where all the rich people wanted to live, Mr. Halston sold all the property he'd bought for like twenty times what he paid for it. He was really lucky, I guess."

"Ah," Sasha said neutrally. "Sure looks like it." He pulled up to the front entrance of Riley's mansion.

"Wait." I belatedly thought through the story with my newly working brain. "It wasn't luck at all, was it? He knew the Department would be securing the Quarter. Maybe he was even part of making that decision."

Sasha turned off his car and shrugged. "Either way—he sounds pretty lucky to me."

Evelyn's distaste for Riley's father suddenly made a lot more sense to me. "Oh my God," I said. "I can't believe I never realized—"

A big man in a black tuxedo tapped on Sasha's window. He was dressed like a waiter, but he had a submachine gun cradled in his left elbow.

"Good evening," he said cheerfully. "Afraid you guys can't park here tonight. There's a spillover parking lot around the corner. Make sure you have your ID handy when you get out of the car."

Sasha nodded and, in a cloud of French-fry fumes, restarted the car. We found the small visitors' parking lot tucked just behind a grove of elm trees. As we parked, Gabriella arrived in Tim Donaldson's car. She was dressed in a kind of sexy-witch costume—a low-cut black dress topped with a big black hat and a white wig. She waved excitedly at me as I got out of the car. "Lauren!" she said. "I didn't know you were coming. Awesome costume!"

She didn't mean it about the costume, but she really was happy to see me.

A few more tuxedoed security guards waited in the parking lot to check our identification and make sure no one tried to bring any weapons in. Two of them frisked Tim and Sasha, while a third argued with a kid who wanted to keep his handgun. Gabriella and I were waved on without being frisked, maybe because we were girls, maybe because the guards recognized us. We waited for Sasha and Tim at the start of the path leading toward Riley's house.

"Are you and Sasha together, Lauren?" Gabriella asked, taking my arm.

"Yeah. He gave me a ride." I deliberately misinterpreted her question, mostly because I didn't know the answer.

"No. I mean are you guys like . . ."

"I don't know."

"It kind of looks like you're together." She surprised me by giving me a hug. She smelled mildly of perfume—the same Marc Jacobs Daisy perfume she'd been wearing for special occasions since we were in ballet together in first grade. "It's good to see you out with a guy. Weird, but good."

Tears sprang into my eyes. I know I've talked a lot about how fake Gabriella and Riley are, but to them it must seem that their sweet old friend has disappeared, replaced by a moody, not-very-nice impostor. And here Gabriella was, being totally sincere about wishing me well anyway. "Good to see you, too," I said. "Are you and Tim back together?"

She rolled her eyes. "Haven't decided yet. He's all over me tonight, but I think it might just be because Lydia dumped him and he's horny."

I shook my head. "No way. Even when he was going out with Lydia, he was always looking at you."

"Seriously?"

I nodded. Tim was kind of dumb, but he was good-looking enough, and he was definitely into Gabriella.

Her smile faltered and she leaned toward me. "Be careful of Sasha," she said in a low voice. "I heard he works for the Department."

"I know," I whispered back. "I'm just using him for his body."

She looked shocked. Then we both laughed, even though I, for one, wasn't so sure I was joking.

The guards finished frisking Sasha and Tim, and we all walked to Riley's house. I've probably been to Riley's house hundreds of times, but this was the first time since my operation, and it seemed different to me. Bigger, fancier.

Tonight there were jack-o'-lanterns lining both sides of the path to the house. I stopped to scrape my fingernail on one of them to make sure. Real pumpkins. God knew where Riley had gotten this many.[15]

---

[15] Up until the first uprising in 2025, many Americans observed a tradition of carving jack-o'-lantern faces into pumpkins for Halloween. The idea was, you'd hollow out a pumpkin and carve a face into its surface. Then, on the night of Halloween, you'd light a candle within the pumpkin, so the jack-o'-lantern face would appear to glow from within. Following the first uprising, laws were passed requiring all farmers who grew

Beyond the pumpkins the big old trees in the yard were hung with green and yellow lights. Sounds of music and people talking wafted from the house, along with the smells of wood-burning fireplaces. A clutch of people stood smoking tobacco and marijuana cigarettes just outside the front door.

We walked into the house and Riley swept up to us. She gave me and Gabriella a big hug. "Lauren! It's so great you made it." Funny thing was, she was being sincere. She'd had a few drinks and they seemed to have washed away a lot of her usual phoniness. She waved at Sasha and Tim. "Did you guys all come together?"

"I drove Tim," Gabriella offered. "And Lauren got a ride with Sasha."

"Cool." Riley's gaze raced between me and Sasha, obviously with the same question Gabriella had asked a few minutes before. "Glad you all made it. Lauren and Gabriella can show you boys around. The main points are: Bands that way." She pointed beyond us to what her family called the Great Hall. "Food in there." She pointed to the living room to our right. "Actually, food and drink are pretty much everywhere."

"My kind of party!" Sasha said.

Riley laughed. "And some more performances and stuff upstairs."

"decorative" crops (including the sorts of pumpkins that made good jack-o'-lanterns) to switch to fuel and food crops. By 2031 only the very wealthy (and shameless) would have even one real jack-o'-lantern on their front porch, let alone the dozens of them that Riley had apparently put out.

148

A bunch of male voices approached behind us. "Good lord." Riley's eyes widened. "I didn't know *he* was coming. I . . . Excuse me." She rushed past us.

We all turned and watched her greet Handsome Hansel Etgar, the video/music/everything star. It was hard to make out if Etgar was as gorgeous as he was supposed to be. He was wearing big sunglasses and surrounded by half a dozen scowling gangster security guards. His guards all seemed twitchy and irritated, probably at having been forced to surrender their guns at the door. They made way for Riley, closing ranks behind her, until all we could see were the District gang signs stenciled on the backs of their leather jackets.

"Well," Gabriella said. "That was our two seconds with Riley for the night." She studied the backs of Etgar's security guys. "Do you think he really recruited his guards from District gangs?"

"Who cares?" Sasha said. "Let's find the food."

We walked into the living room and found—as promised—that there was food and drink everywhere. The walls of the living room had been covered with fake cobwebs that shimmered in the strobe lights. Gabriella moved off to say hi to Charlotte Montauk and some of her other friends, while Sasha picked up a few pieces of sushi and thrust them into his mouth.

He saw me watching. "Didn't have dinner tonight," he said around a mouthful of food. He said it cheerfully enough, but there was an undertone to his voice that made me remember the boxes of macaroni and cheese I'd seen in the recycling bin on his porch.

"Does anyone else live in Mazen's house with you?" I asked.

"Mazen?"

"The house where you live—does anyone else live there?"

Sasha shook his head, jaws still working. "Nah. I'm a lone wolf." He howled softly and shrugged. "They haven't sent me out with a handler since I was twelve. They used to shop for me, but that stopped once I got old enough to drive."

"Sympathetic backstory?" I asked.

"Sure. Also happens to be true." He took a few more pieces of sushi. "Excuse me. I have work to do." He scanned the room, jaw working, and made his way to the next table of food, this one laden with Middle Eastern dips and pita.

I watched him make his way from table to table—from meze to grilled shrimp to sausage to pastries and so on. Gabriella and Melissa Spindle found me standing there alone. Gabriella handed me a glass of punch. "Did your boyfriend abandon you for the food?"

"Kind of looks like that." I realized they were both grinning at me and quickly added, "Not that he's my boyfriend." I had a small sip of the punch. It tasted like pineapple juice with a slight alcoholic aftertaste.

Across the hall I saw some of the guys laughing and passing a small pillbox around. "Keep an eye on your cups," I told Gabriella and Melissa. "I'm pretty sure they brought something to spike the drinks with."

Gabriella surprised me by laughing. "As though they'd share," Gabriella said. "Xavier Neufeld brought some E-Love, but only for his paying customers."

Melissa elbowed me gently. "You've gotten paranoid, Lauren."

"Yep," I said. What I didn't understand was why everyone wasn't feeling more paranoid, what with the surveillance cameras scattered around the room, plus the tuxedoed security guards muttering into their headsets, not to mention the glowering gangster types who had come in with Etgar. Still, I forced myself to smile with my friends. I wanted to at least look like I was having fun.

I kept half an eye on Sasha as he circulated to each and every food table.

I don't know where Etgar had got off to, but a few of his security gangsters had established themselves around the guacamole. Avocados are so expensive these days that serving real guacamole is sort of like serving cake with real gold in the icing (which Riley also does at these parties). Sasha squeezed past one of the gangsters, an enormous white guy with a shaved head and teardrop tattoos on both cheeks.

Sasha was so focused on filling his plate with guacamole he didn't seem to notice the guy's casually murderous glare. Then, backing up, he glanced at the guy, stumbled, and spilled his entire plate of guacamole on the guy's pants.

The guy looked down incredulously at the green mess dripping off the crotch of his pants.

I happened to be standing where I had a good view of Sasha's face. He imitated the guy's expression so well I couldn't help smiling. The guy went from incredulous to violent in about half a second. He started to reach inside his jacket where his gun would ordinarily have been, remembered he'd surrendered his gun, and punched Sasha in the face, then in the stomach, then—when Sasha started bending over—in the face again.

Sasha went down hard, his glasses cracking and falling off his face, his nose bleeding.

I don't remember moving, but suddenly I was across the room standing between Sasha and the security gangsters. In front of me the big bald gangster guy was clutching his throat and bent over. I guess I might have punched him in the throat and then kicked him between the legs. His friends were massing around him, obviously wanting to kick someone's butt, but not quite ready to attack a sixteen-year-old girl. Or maybe just too conscious of how out-gunned they were. Then Riley's security men were everywhere, Tasers out, faces grim.

In the end, no one got Tasered. No one got shot. The guy who'd hit Sasha allowed himself to be led out of the party, while the rest of Etgar's security melted away, presumably to re-form around Etgar himself. Someone got Sasha some ice for his nose.

Sasha's glasses were totally unsalvageable. They'd fallen off his face and, in the chaos, someone (I presumed Sasha, but maybe one of the quasi-gangsters had done it for him) had crushed them.

I stood next to Sasha as he filled a new plate at the seafood table. "Thanks," he said. "The guy was about to stamp on my face when you got in his way."

"Wasn't there a less painful way to get your glasses—"

"Hey," he interrupted, and I remembered that the security guys surrounding us were all working for the Department. "Are you okay with driving us home?"

"Not really. Why?"

He blinked a few times, forehead crinkling. "I can barely see across the room now."

"You really need glasses to see? I figured they were just for the Department to—"

"Nope. I'm super-nearsighted, and go figure—the Department has never offered to pay for the eye operation. So can you drive home?"

"I guess. No stupider than anything else I have planned for tonight."

Sasha smiled and took my arm. "I can't see squat, so you'll have to be my guide to the party. Tell me if we pass anyone I should say hi to." In a lower voice, lips so close to my ear I could feel his breath, he said, "Clock's ticking. I'm supposed to be on my way home right now, so I can boot up my backup glasses as quickly as possible. Where are we going?"

I led him toward the Great Hall. "Not too fast," he cautioned, lips brushing my ear. "We're just ambling through the party." He smiled at some guy who happened to catch his eye, and waved at someone else.

We made our way through the dance floor, Sasha clasping the hands of anyone he recognized, bumping chests, etc. For all the world just the cool new kid having a good time at a party. The only false note: the bruises coming up on his face.

I couldn't quite imitate his nonchalance, but I slowed to his pace and smiled at anyone I recognized.

We passed Riley dancing with a very good-looking guy I'd never seen before. She waved me over. I mouthed *bathroom* and kept walking.

Finally we made it to the base of the main staircase. We picked our way past the handful of kids sitting on the enormous stairs. Upstairs, a dozen or so people were watching a movie in Riley's home theater, while a few more were wandering around trying the locked doors to the bedrooms, maybe looking for another bathroom. We weren't the only couple up there either—at least three couples had given up on finding more privacy and were making out in the darker corners of the hallway.

I led Sasha down the hall to the back staircase. A tuxedoed waiter walked out of the stairwell, balancing a tray of drinks on one hand. He carefully closed the door behind him, making sure the lock engaged, before walking past us.

Once the waiter was past, Sasha waved his wand at the lock. "Alohomora!" he said.

I glanced at him, puzzled.

"Sorry. Harry Potter joke. It's the magic spell that . . . Forget it." Sasha tried the door handle. "Do you have a way of getting the door open?"

"Hopefully." I flipped open the numeric keypad next to the fingerprint lock. "Assuming they haven't changed the servants' code in the last few months . . ." I punched the numbers: 1-0-3-0. Riley's birthday. A small click, and I pushed the door open. The back staircase was much less fancy than the main one: tiled steps, exposed brick wall bare except for lights and surveillance cameras.

I ran up the stairs, averting my face from the cameras and clutching Sasha's hand in mine. With any luck, whoever was watching the cameras would miss us. They had a lot to watch tonight. If they did see us, hopefully they'd just assume we were sneaking off to make out in privacy, now that Sasha's glasses had been disabled. We emerged in a hallway on the third floor, a few yards from Riley's rooms. I glanced down the hall toward her father's office. The door was closed, but a little light bled out from beneath it.

"In here." I led him into Riley's art room/office. As usual, her desk was barely visible beneath a pile of clothes and other crap. I pushed a pair of jeans out of the way and opened the desk's top drawer. It was filled to bursting: hair ties, lipstick, perfume, vitamins, and so on. I picked up two big handfuls of stuff and put them on the floor, trying to keep everything more or less together.

I turned back to the desk drawer, sifting through what was left. What if Riley had started keeping the whistle somewhere else? What if she had thrown it out? I took out a box of colored pencils. Three pads of sticky notes. An energy bar. A box of birth control pills.

Sasha's phone buzzed. He glanced at it, tapped out a quick message, and put it back in his pocket. "My handler's getting impatient."

"Him and me both," I said. There wasn't much left in the drawer now. An old tablet computer. A silver frame with a picture of Riley and her parents in their old front yard. Damn damn damn.

"What are you looking for?" Sasha asked.

"A way to get her father out of his office," I said. I picked up the picture frame, and finally, there it was, wedged in the corner of the drawer. A small green whistle. I closed my hand around it. I smiled.

"Ah, so we can use his computer?"

"Exactly." I showed Sasha the whistle. "He's going to take his dog for a quick walk."

It was a scheme Riley came up with when she was ten, crafty little girl that she was. Every time she blew the whistle she gave her father's Pomeranian a treat. Cedar's not a stupid dog. It didn't take him long to start scratching on the office door every time Riley blew the dog whistle.

I opened Riley's door a crack so I could see down the hallway to where her dad's office was. I brought the whistle to my mouth and blew.

No movement from the office. I listened hard, but the music downstairs was too loud for me to hear a dog scratching at the door. Shoot. Maybe it had been so long that Cedar didn't care about the whistle anymore. I blew the whistle again. Waited twenty seconds. Blew it again.

Finally the door to Riley's father's office opened. Mr. Halston stood silhouetted, Cedar panting at his side. "For God's sake, Cedar. You have to pee more often than I do." Riley's father ambled toward the servants' staircase, one hand in Cedar's thick fur. "We'll go out the back way. God forbid Riley's friends see any evidence she has a parent."

I stepped farther into Riley's room, holding my breath, until I heard the door to the servants' staircase close behind Mr. Halston.

The moment the door closed, I led Sasha toward the office. "Come on. Before the server logs him out for inactivity." I ran down the hallway and lunged across Mr. Halston's office to tap at his keyboard and keep the connection alive.

Sasha slid into Mr. Halston's desk chair and started pulling up menus on the computer's screen, leaning in so he could see the screen without his glasses. "You're a genius," he said. He waved a hand at the retinal scanner and the security fob mount. "Triple-factor authentication, and we didn't even need a password." He opened up a server and began sifting through folders. "Why did Riley have a dog whistle in her desk?"

"Sometimes she wanted her dad out of his office."

"Yeah, I got that. But why?"

"You know how it is . . ." I stopped myself, realizing that Sasha really didn't know. How old had he been when the Department had found him in the refugee camp? Did he even remember his parents? "Growing up, sometimes you want your father to stop working. Riley's father has always worked a lot." I felt a pang of guilt, thinking of ten-year-old Riley staring at her father's office door, blowing her stupid dog whistle, waiting for him to come out. Hoping he'd notice her.

Sasha met my eyes. "Betraying your friends isn't so fun, is it? I usually tell myself that I don't have a choice. That I have to do it."

"But I don't *have* to do it," I said. "I could just live in ignorance."

"That's the problem," Sasha said. "You almost never *have* to do anything." He hesitated. "Do you want me to stop?"

I didn't hesitate. "I want you to hurry up. Cedar's too old to go for long walks."

Sasha turned back to the screen so quickly, I wondered if he'd have stopped if I told him to. "We'll be done in a minute. This guy has crazy-good access." He clicked through a few more folders and typed *Fie* in a search dialogue. "Here you are: Fielding, Lauren, 349205." He put out his hand. "Nano drive, please."

I took the ancient nano drive out of my pocket and handed it to him.

He leaned over the computer and inserted the drive. "Thanks for grabbing this. I didn't want to have to explain why I had it in my pocket when the guards frisked me."

"You think they would have cared about a nano drive?"

"You can't be too careful," he said, straightening up. "When you're about to do something totally dumb, I mean. Here we go."

He sat back in the desk chair and dragged a bunch of folders onto the nano drive's icon. Standing, he plucked the nano drive from Mr. Halston's device and handed it to me. "And there you are."

He turned back to the screen. "Let me back out of here, and we can go." As he spoke, his fingers continued to fly over the computer's screen. I might not have noticed what he did next if his shoulders hadn't suddenly tensed. Even so, I almost missed the moment when he deleted my folders, taking them permanently off the Department's system.

"Whoa!" I hit Sasha's shoulder. "Why'd you do that? They'll know someone broke into their system and deleted my files."

He didn't answer. His face was oddly still as he stared at the screen, fingers still flying over the keyboard. "They won't notice for a while," he said. "I created some dummy folders. Assuming no one tries to open them in the next few hours, when the backup servers do their sync tonight, your backup files will be written over, too."

"But why?"

He shut down the folder he was looking at and brought up the spreadsheet Mr. Halston had had up when he left the room. "Would you believe me if I told you I'm protecting you?"

"No. I would not."

He glanced at me. "So call it a side project. Don't ask more if you don't want me to lie." He rose. "We should get back."

I put the drive in my pocket, following him out of the office. "Why would someone at the Department ask you to delete Departmental data?" He didn't have to answer. No one at the Department would ask that. Of course they wouldn't. "Shoot. You're subcontracting, aren't you?"

His left cheek gave a minuscule twitch. "Stop it," he said. "I did what you wanted me to. Leave the rest alone. I assure you that the person who asked me to delete your data has no interest in the Department finding out what we did tonight."

"Who are you selling my files to?"

"I don't have your files," Sasha said. "You have them in your pocket. All I did was delete the Department's copy."

"For who?" I demanded. "Those are the records of my life! Who wanted you to delete them?"

We heard steps in the stairwell, and both our heads swiveled toward the door. Someone opened the downstairs door, and we heard the distant voices of servants carrying out more party supplies.

"We should go," Sasha said. "And you should keep your voice down."

I darted into Riley's room and put everything back in her desk drawer. Casting a quick look around the room's mess, I was pretty sure Riley wouldn't notice anything out of place.

I rejoined Sasha in the hallway, and together we entered the servants' stairwell. We were walking down the stairs, back under the surveillance cameras, when he paused. He turned to me, and I realized he was angry, too, or at least defensive. Keeping the back of his head to the camera, he said, "What would *you* do to get out of being a human surveillance camera? Recording every interaction you have with everyone and anyone you meet? I have to apply for a special permit from my handler to take my glasses off at any point between six a.m. and ten p.m. Seven days a week. And that assumes I'm in bed at ten. If I stay up later, the glasses stay on later."

I didn't say anything.

"That time I met you in the tree house—that was the only unmonitored interaction I've had with another person in over a year. You know how I got there *without* my glasses? I pretended to go to sleep and then climbed out the bedroom window."

I thought of that night. The heat of his lips in the chilly air.

"Then, the next day and the day after, I couldn't talk to you about what happened between us. I couldn't say a thing to you without everyone at work hearing every word. You have no idea how much I want to just have a private conversation with you."

I stepped toward him, in full view of the surveillance camera, and kissed him. He froze for a second, his face strangely naked without his glasses, then kissed me back.

It felt very different from making out in the darkness of the tree house. The staircase was brightly lit with fluorescent light, and at any moment someone could have interrupted us. The nearest security camera was maybe five feet away and pointing straight at us. And still, it was two or three minutes before I pulled away.

Sasha kept his arms around me and, lips near my ear, muttered, "Was that just to convince security we weren't up to anything serious upstairs?"

"Why else would I kiss you?" I whispered back as I took his hand and led him down the stairs. The party was in full swing when we emerged from the back staircase. A DJ had set up in the home theater, and the second floor was full of people dancing now, too.

I looked around for Riley and Gabriella, wanting to say goodbye, but the place was thronged. It was all we could do to make our way down the main stairs toward the front door.

We stepped outside, into a cloud of tobacco and marijuana smoke. I took out my cell phone and texted Riley a quick apology for not saying goodbye before we left.

We got back to the car, both of us still jittery with excitement.

Sasha took my hand, and I leaned toward him. "Maybe we don't have to go straight home," I said.

He kissed me. A quick, chaste touch of our lips. Then he met my eyes, sighed, and handed me the car keys. "I have to get my backup pair of glasses on. Or we're gonna catch someone's attention."

I glanced down at the keys, puzzled.

"You're driving me home," Sasha said. "I can't see squat."

"Oh. Right." I walked around the car and sat in the driver's seat. I held the keys toward the ignition and the car purred to life, the smell of slightly burnt French fries filling the air.

"Now what?" I said, once Sasha had folded himself into the passenger seat.

"Now you take me home."

"No. I mean, how do I back up?"

He stared at me, comprehension slowly dawning on his face. "Wait. You've *never* driven before?"

"I have a disability," I said. "At least I used to. I wasn't even supposed to cross the street on my own. You think they were going to let me drive?" I looked at the gearshift and saw the letters there. "How hard can it be? I assume *R* is for reverse." I tried pulling the gearshift toward the *R* but it didn't move.

"You have to hold the button in," Sasha said, then put his hand over my hand to prevent me switching gears. "Okay. Let's switch places. I'll drive."

"You can't see."

"And you can't drive. I'll be fine. Probably."

We switched places, and he backed the car out of its parking spot, hunched forward, squinting over the wheel like an old man. Once we made it to the highway, he relaxed a little as the car's autodriver took over.

Getting from the highway's exit to our subdivision was more sketchy.

The car's ancient safety features were all that saved us. It abruptly braked half a dozen times when Sasha was about to rear-end the car ahead of us, and several times swerved itself back to the center of our lane, when Sasha drifted toward opposing traffic. Fortunately, it was almost 11 p.m. on a Saturday, and the suburban streets were quiet.

When we finally got to his house, he jumped out of the car. "Let me get my glasses back on. Then I'll give you a lift home."

"I live two blocks away. I'll walk." It was still a thrill to me—walking around by myself at night. "Unless . . . Did you want to open the files with me?"

He inhaled sharply, then shook his head. "I can't. My handler knows I'm home. He'll go crazy if I don't get my glasses back on." He smiled at me—the kind of sweet, sad smile that would have melted my brain if I had let it. I didn't let it. "You'll have to fill me in. I trust you."

His words hung there for a moment, as awkward as if he'd just confessed his undying love to me. Because I sure don't trust him. Like him, yes. Desire him, definitely. But trust . . . ? I'm not an idiot anymore.

"Sure," I said after the moment had become thoroughly awkward. "I'll tell you all about it tomorrow."

"In the tree house?" he said. "Ten thirty tomorrow night?"

"As close to that as I can get out." I started to walk away. At the same moment he started to come around the car toward me.

We both froze, then he continued toward me. His hands were cold, his lips warm. "This was a really fun date," he said a few seconds later.

I snorted. But he was right, it really had been fun. My first date ever. "See you tomorrow," I said.

I walked home, feeling happy and nervous, one hand cradling the nano drive in my pocket. As far as I could tell, we had gotten away with something we had no business getting away with.

My mother was waiting up for me in the living room. "Did Sasha drop you off?" she asked.

I shook my head. "I walked from his house. He got his glasses broken at the party, so we had to stop at his place first."

She kissed my cheek. "Did you have fun?"

"Sure. We didn't stay long, because of his glasses, but it was fun."

"What happened to his glasses?"

Before I could answer, Evelyn came down the stairs dressed for bed. "You okay?" she said.

"Sure!" I found myself slipping back into my old perky tone, as much to reassure myself as them. "I love Riley's Halloween parties."

"I like them much more now that I don't have to go." Evelyn examined me, suddenly seeming uncertain. "Sasha was . . . nice?"

I nodded. "I know he's an agent for the Department, Ev. But

Sasha and I understand each other. You should be more careful around Peter, though."

Evelyn frowned. "You too?"

"Your father and Evelyn had a big fight about Peter earlier," my mother said. "Your father says hello, by the way. He'll be back tomorrow evening."

"I'm not going to abandon Peter—" Evelyn started.

"I don't care if you abandon him," I said. "Just don't say anything incriminating around him. The guy would narc on you in a heartbeat."

"Is that what your boyfriend said? He would know."

She meant it as an insult, but she was absolutely right. It *was* what Sasha had said, and he *would* know. I gave her a hug. "Just because Peter went to jail doesn't mean you should, Evelyn."

Even writing this on a safe computer with no immediate intention to send it to anyone, I'm reading this over to make sure there's not the slightest hint of anything seditious in Evelyn's words. She's trying to be a loyal friend to Peter, that's all.

I said good night to my mother and Evelyn and walked upstairs. Leaving my lights off, I slotted the nano drive into this old laptop. And that's where the good part of my night ended.

Dr. Corbin, I don't understand the science, not really, though it seems that you did something impressive. Not just garden-variety genetic manipulation. I'm sure you're very proud of yourself.

Sad thing is, it turns out it's too late for me to do anything to stop you. Killing myself a few months ago—now that would have put a serious crimp in your plans. It's a tough realization—knowing that nothing I do now could possibly accomplish as much as dying before the operation.

But that's . . . what's the expression? A day too late and a dollar too little.

It's 1:30 a.m., and my head hurts. So I'm going to sleep. Don't worry, Dr. Corbin. Tomorrow I'll come back and edit this into a journal entry I can send you. I'll take out the bits about the Department's database, and make up some stuff about how Sasha and I made wild, passionate love on Riley's bed. I may need to look up some of the technical details about the lovemaking, but I'm sure I can figure out something juicy and plausible. Maybe even a little acrobatic.

Then I'll write up a real journal entry about what I found. Not for you, Dr. Corbin, but for someone else. Hopefully lots of someones, if things ever get desperate enough for me to post this online.

> Not-so-sincerely
> yours,
> Lauren

Video Clip #1

Caption: Innocence Treatment

Experimental testing protocol #0239A67

Recorded October 8, 2031, at the Department's

detention facility in San Luis Obispo, California.

Description:

A young man in a maroon T-shirt sits at a steel table. His eyes are red-rimmed and his nose is running, likely with the aftereffects of tear gas. He's in his early twenties—maybe even younger.[16]

---

[16] I've been unable to conclusively identify the prisoner, despite a good deal of effort. The interviewer refers to him as "Mr. Palmer," but there is no record of someone with that last name being held at the San Luis Obispo Detention Facility in 2031. (Given how heavily redacted the Department's records are from that time, this by no means precludes that a

"You have no excuse for holding me," he tells someone offscreen. "I was participating in a peaceful protest. What am I charged with?"

"You're not charged with anything, Mr. Palmer," the offscreen interviewer answers. "Rather, you're helping the march of progress. You've been recruited into a small experiment the Department is running at this facili—"

"I'm not taking part in any experiment. I want to see a lawyer."

"Let me start by asking: what do you think of the government?"

"I have nothing to say. Not until I see a lawyer."

"After this experiment—which should take no more than a few hours—the Department will release you, with no charges and with no additional consequences."

Palmer stares into the camera. He says nothing.

After a moment the interviewer says, "I just told you that we'll be releasing you soon. Do you believe me?"

Palmer's lips thin. "Of course not."

"And—finally—please give me a list of the protest's other organizers."

Palmer rubs his reddened eyes. "I'm not giving you names," he says. Not defiant, but resigned. "Do what you want to me, but I'm not giving you a single name."

Palmer was involved in an experiment at the facility—it just means I cannot substantiate his identity.)

The interviewer makes a sound that could be a laugh, could be a cough. "Excellent," he says. "So concludes the first part of our time together. Baseline responses are established. Go on."

A gray-clad guard appears in the camera frame, back of his head to the camera. In his hand he's holding a small plastic container with a spray top—like a bottle of cheap perfume. Palmer looks afraid, but he doesn't move as the guard brings the bottle toward him and sprays him full in the face.

At the last second Palmer closes his eyes and brings up his hands, but he still gets a faceful of the spray. "Not a single name," he repeats.

The interviewer says nothing. In the corner of the screen a little digital clock appears and starts ticking down from thirty. By the time it hits zero, Palmer is sitting up straighter in his chair, his eyes wide.

"All right," the interviewer says. "Please tell me what you think of the government."

"It's a kleptocracy," Palmer says immediately. "A government made of thieves, each desperate to get their own slice before things fall apart for good."

"Hmm," the interviewer says. "I completely agree with you. I have good news. There are going to be elections in three months. No big campaign donations will be allowed. We expect an entirely new government by February."

Palmer's face breaks into a huge smile.

"That's why we took you in," the interviewer says. "Just to let you know. Could you tell us the names and addresses of everyone you can remember who feels like you do about the current government? We want to get in touch with them and let them know the good news."

"Oh my lord!" Palmer says, grinning like he's won the lottery. "I want to call them right now."

"Get him the phone," the interviewer calls to someone. (Or, more likely, to no one at all.) He shoves a pad of paper onto the table in front of Palmer and hands him a pen. "Why don't you write their names down while we're waiting for the phone? We don't want to forget anyone."

Palmer leans over the pad of paper and starts to write, smiling in anticipation of how happy his friends will be to get the news.

Caption: Two hours later—post-treatment interview.
Palmer is still behind the steel table, slumped in his chair, gray-faced with exhaustion or despair. Or both.

"Mr. Palmer," the interviewer says. "I want to ask you a few more questions and then, I promise you, your part in this experiment is over. What do you think of the United States government?"

Palmer shakes his head and mutters, "You bastards drugged me. So what? That's not admissible in court."

"Hmm. And would you care to confirm the list of like-minded individuals you provided?"

Palmer wipes his face, still staring at the table. "Go to hell. They were just people who popped into my head. Nothing to do with the democracy movement."

"And, finally, when do you anticipate being released?" the interviewer asks.

At this Palmer looks directly at the interviewer. "Whenever you damn well please," he says.

Fade to black. An appended data file notes that "post-intervention" medical tests showed no identifiable chemical signature in the subject's body.

Additional Comments:

There are three other video clips much like this one. A would-be suicide bomber is easily convinced to provide a list of his handlers and their contact information. A drug boss turns over detailed access information on the investment accounts where he's laundered his illicit fortune. An illegal immigrant volunteers the names, addresses, and jobs of a dozen family members, also in the country illegally.

The format is the same in each video: an individual is sprayed (with what one presumes is an aerosol version of the Innocence Treatment) and quickly becomes so gullible that they are easily induced to act against their own, or their group's, self-interest. (As a researcher, of course, I wonder if there were other test subjects whom the treatment affected less. I can easily imagine Paxeon exaggerating the treatment's impact in order to excite their Departmental sponsors.)

If you'd like to watch any or all of these videos yourself, they are readily available online (though I strongly suggest you anonymize your computer before watching them). In the interests of brevity, I'm only describing one more video clip at length. This final clip is quite different from the others, veering away from experimental verification and toward marketing. It's worth considering, if only as evidence of how the Department intended to monetize its investment in the Innocence Treatment.

Video Clip #5

Caption: Innocence Treatment
Proof of concept, worker pacification

Description:
A silver-haired white man stands behind a lectern, beaming at the camera (and at his presumed audience of CEOs
and government officials). "Does your company struggle
with the consequences of low worker morale? Absenteeism,
worker theft, labor organizing? They all have the same
root cause—your workers don't trust you to do what's best
for them. What if you could convince them?"

He snaps his fingers and the screen fills with images
of Chinese workers filing into a large warehouse space
filled with what looks like voting booths. "The following
is real-life footage of a recent experiment carried out

with workers in a factory in Shenzhen, China. The factory does high-end fabrication for some of the world's most successful electronic companies.

"First, workers were surveyed anonymously about their feelings for their employer."

Caption: The proportion of workers who expressed high levels of trust in their employer was less than 20 percent.

"Next, workers were exposed to our patented trust-enhancing chemical regime. The treatment is odorless and takes only a few seconds to administer to hundreds of workers."

An image of workers assembled in a smaller room, presumably to economize on the amount of Innocence Treatment necessary to reach them. A barely audible hiss as a mist comes through the vents. The men and women look around, worried for an instant. Suddenly animated, they exchange words in a southern dialect of Mandarin Chinese peppered with English slang.

The door opens and the workers walk back to the voting booths, presumably to fill out a post-treatment survey.

Caption: The proportion of workers in the experimental group who expressed high levels of trust in their employer more than tripled.

The video moves on to show the workers hard at work. One employee is filmed doing something complicated with a 3-D printer while two others lean over a large touch screen, collaborating. They all look happy.

"Our treatment improves morale without degrading workers' abilities to accomplish complex tasks. The effects will entirely dissipate by the end of the shift, leaving the workers ignorant that they've been exposed to anything at all. Don't take our word for it. Contact us for a free trial."

The Paxeon logo floats across the screen, while in the background the workers continue to demonstrate their productivity.

"Paxeon Solutions. Making change profitable."

JOURNAL OF
LAUREN C. FIELDING

Sunday, November 2, 2031

Dear Dr. Corbin (or, okay, whoever actually ends up reading this):

This morning, when I was changing my last journal entry into something I could send to you, I realized that I never said what I actually found out last night. To anyone who ends up reading my journal: sorry about that. I wasn't deliberately keeping anything back. It was more that writing it down seemed like it would somehow make it more true. And I don't want it to be true.

But, shoot. What's the point of keeping a journal if you're not going to be honest, right? And if I ever do wind up posting this online, I want people to know what you did, Dr. Corbin. Not the details (which are totally beyond me), but the gist: you took my parents' genetic material and twisted it. Not to make me super-strong or smart or anything fun, but to make me useful.

It turns out it's really hard—almost impossible with existing technologies—to make a new chemical compound with predictable effects on the human brain. The brain is a subtle place, I guess, and even the most sophisticated computer is better at replicating human proteins than making new ones.

So you did what you had to, Dr. Corbin. Or what you wanted to, anyway. You engineered my genes so that when my brain was developing I would make a new kind of brain cell. From the moment I was conceived in your laboratory, my brain didn't just make all the usual white- and gray-matter cells that people use to think. It made all those, but it also made one additional type of brain cell. In your return-on-investment statement (thoughtfully kept in the Department's file on me) you called it the "Innocence Treatment." Nice name, by the way. Much catchier than the technical term, which, if I read the files right, is "modified oligodendrocytes."[17]

This "treatment" was the reason I used to be the way that I was—I was so awash in the additional type of brain cell that my brain could barely function. Once you were sure the cells were stable, you could extract them, study their cellular structure, and figure out how to encourage normal people's brains to

---

[17] A decade later, Paxeon and the Department continue to deny the existence of the Innocence Treatment, so the scientific details remain obscure, with no publicly accessible research on the topic. That said, advances in brain mapping and genome mapping in the early part of this century made this sort of project the subject of speculation as early as 2014. (See Corbin, Stein, et al., "Gene Structure and Oligodendrocyte Production," *Journal of Brain Science* 304 (2014): 520–528.)

make that kind of brain cell. I still don't know if taking out all the weird cells just happened to fix my brain, or if you fixed me on purpose and this is an additional experiment that I'm experiencing now.

No big mystery why the Department would be interested in the Innocence Treatment. I can imagine the folks in charge drooling at the thought of a drug that turns *anyone* into a cheerful informant (with no Rule #7 to keep their mouths shut).

I *could* imagine that, but I don't have to—I can just watch a video. Thank you, Department! They've already gone ahead and tested it on a bunch of prisoners, recording the results just in case some foreign dictator didn't get exactly how useful the Innocence Treatment would be to them. Those were the videos I couldn't stop watching last night.

So that's what I found—the purpose of my life was to be a petri dish, growing a chemical that temporarily turns people into a replica of the old me. Stupid. Pliable. Happy.

I spent most of today inside, watching old movies. Trying and failing to distract myself. Trying and failing to believe that at least you were done with me, and now I could move on with my life. The problem is, I saw the way you looked at me the other day, and I *know* you're not done with me.

I really felt like spending the night inside, too. I had no desire to go to Sasha's house and tell him that I was a genetically engineered mutant who had already served her purpose, which was to produce a special kind of brain cell. I didn't feel like seeing his face and trying to guess how much he already knew or what he thought of me now.

But a deal's a deal. I slipped out of my house just after 10 p.m.

It was harder to get out this time. Every time I opened my bedroom door, I found Evelyn at her desk across the hall, door open, chair half turned to face the hallway. I think she's trying to keep track of me, worried that I've gotten involved in something over my head with Sasha. Which is kind of right, except that it's not really about Sasha and I've been involved since the moment I was conceived.

I eventually went downstairs. Evelyn came with me. I pretended I was hungry and got myself a snack. She had a snack, too. I went back upstairs, and she went back upstairs to her room and resumed reading, door still open, her chair still facing the hall. I could have just told her I was going out, I guess, but I didn't want to tell her about the Innocence Treatment, and I didn't want her getting our parents involved.

Plus, sneaking out my window seemed like a lot more fun than walking out the front door.

I locked the door to my room and opened my window. It was a cool night, so I quickly pulled on a fleece before poking my head out the window. There's a little ledge beneath my window, shingled with solar panels, then another ten feet or so to the ground. Ten feet. Too far to jump.

I stripped my bed, tied the sheets together, and secured one end of the sheet rope to my desk. After tossing the other end out the window, I climbed out myself and gently sat down on the ledge of solar panels.

Then, very slowly easing my legs over the lip of the ledge, I climbed down the sheet until my whole body was dangling in the air. I had another foot or so of sheet to go when I heard a ripping sound from above me. I bent my knees and let go.

I hit the grass next to my house and fell forward. The grass was moist with dew, the ground hard and cold. I got to my feet and brushed myself off. My knees and wrist hurt where I'd fallen on them, but they weren't too bad. I heard nothing from inside the house. No windows opened. No one thundered down the stairs to stop me.

Keeping to the shadows, I ran through our neighbors' backyard before emerging on the street a few houses down. Just like the last time I snuck out to meet Sasha, being outside at night on my own lifted my spirits. I didn't run this time. I walked slowly, appreciating every step of my freedom. My whole existence might be due to Corbin's nasty little plan to make nasty little chemicals, but tonight, at least, I was free.

This time, I didn't look in people's windows. Instead, I kept to the darkest patches I could find. It was a clear night overhead and after my eyes adjusted to the darkness I could see the stars. I found the Big Dipper, or maybe it was the Little Dipper—I don't really know constellations. Still, it was nice to see the stars. In eighth-grade science we learned that it takes centuries for the light from our sun to travel to most of the stars in our galaxy. That might not sound comforting, but it was a comfort to me tonight—the thought that Dr. Corbin and I would both be long dead before the sunlight from today hit most of the stars I was looking at right now.

I found Sasha at the base of the tree, looking around a little anxiously. He relaxed when he saw me. "Hi," he said quietly. "I wasn't sure you were coming."

"I keep my promises."

He grinned. "Yeah, well, don't feel too bad about that. You're still recovering from major brain surgery."

"Funny." I put one hand on his shoulder and hesitated. Somehow in all my brooding about being a human petri dish, I'd forgotten to think about what it would be like to tell Sasha. What would he think of me? Why did I care so much? All my anger at the Department and exhilaration at being out at night and . . . whatever it was that I felt for Sasha . . . it made it hard to think straight. I wanted to kiss him, and I wanted to hit him.

I pointed at the tree house with my free hand. "Race you up?"

He didn't respond, but I read the tension in his body. The instant before he moved, I hip checked him to one side, and leaped up the tree ahead of him.

It wasn't even close. I made it to the tree house at least ten seconds before him. "You win," he said. "So? What did you find?"

The remnants of my good mood vanished. "You must already know," I said. "You deleted the files the Department has on me. I don't see you as a guy who'd delete something without knowing what it is."

He made a face. "Maybe I just knew you'd be telling me tonight."

"I thought you said you weren't sure I'd be coming."

"Did I say that?" he asked. "I was probably just being polite."

I didn't respond, and after a minute, he said, "If I already know, what's the harm in telling me? And anyway, you keep your promises, right?"

I still didn't say anything. Mostly because I really didn't feel like talking about the Innocence Treatment. He waited. I let the silence stretch for a minute or two, the only noise the distant sound of traffic on Bradley Street.

Finally, I took a deep breath and told him. He made surprised sounds and faces in the right places, but I wasn't sure how authentic they were. I still have a hard time telling when Sasha is lying.

I've thought about this a lot, Dr. Corbin, and I think a lot of my new talent for seeing lies is just basically a willingness to be clear-eyed. Maybe not everyone could be quite as "talented" as me, but they could definitely be a little more perceptive if they wanted, don't you think? So I'm not sure if my confusion around Sasha is because he's such a great liar, or if it's just that I like him so much that I *want* to believe him. I want to believe he really likes me.

Sitting next to him in the tree house, I was super-conscious of his nearness. Of his smell, some boy deodorant mixed with the slightly spicy scent of his sweat.

He shook his head when I was done explaining about the Innocence Treatment. "So if that's the big secret, why are they still so interested?" he finally asked.

"You mean, if the whole point of my existence was to produce

chemicals, why are they still following me when I've already pro-
duced those chemicals?"

He gently ran his hand over the stubbled and scarred back of
my head. "Lauren. Just because that's what Corbin was after, that
doesn't make it the whole point of your life."

I leaned against him, embarrassed at how relieved I was that
he wasn't repulsed by me. "Okay," I said, keeping my voice as level
as I could. "So why do you think she's still having me followed?"

"I have no idea," he said. "Scientific curiosity?" His teeth glinted
in the moonlight. "Wondering how anyone can be so hot?"

I laughed despite myself.

Nothing else happened in the tree house tonight that would
matter to someone else. Funny how important something like putting your tongue in another person's mouth can feel when it's happening to you, and how irrelevant (and let's be honest, slightly
gross) it sounds when you're telling someone about it.

It's embarrassing. We'd just been talking about a chemical that
has the power to pretty significantly mess up the world, but for a few
minutes, all I could think about was how Sasha tasted and smelled.

Eventually I tore myself away. I walked home alone, still not
knowing if I could trust Sasha at all. Probably not caring quite as
much as I should.

I got home to find that the sheet I'd left dangling out my window was gone, and the window to my room was shut. Uh-oh.

Shouldn't have been a big deal, right? I'd just discovered that
my life was a side effect of an evil science experiment. Who cared
if I was in trouble with my parents?

Still, I dragged my feet as I walked up the front walkway to my house. I didn't want to tell my parents what I'd discovered. It would make them feel bad, and they couldn't do anything about it, anyway. I wondered if they suspected anything. I figured they had to. I mean, what are the chances that the same doctor who helped them conceive would just happen to be the one who came up with the treatment to fix their daughter?

I opened the front door and found Evelyn sitting on the stairs looking exhausted. "Oh," I said. "Hey!"

"Oh," she said, imitating my perky tone. "Hey!"

I stood there for a moment, and in the same cheery voice, she said, "How's it going?"

"Good." I cautiously started walking up the stairs. "How about you?"

"Great, great! Oh," she said, like she was just remembering. "A weird thing happened before. I heard this thump from your room. Opened the door and—"

"My door was locked."

"Seriously?" she said. "You think Mom and Dad would let you have a room that really locks? You stick the end of a paper clip in the little hole in the doorknob and your door opens right up."

"Oh."

"So I opened the door and you'll never guess what I found."

"I think I might guess," I said.

She smiled a little, then frowned again. "Being the good sister that I am, I went outside, made sure that you weren't lying injured in the yard. Then I went back up to your room, pulled up the sheets,

184

threw out the one you ripped, and remade your bed. I didn't wake up Mom or Dad. Though I would have if you had been out for another thirty minutes."

"Thanks, Ev," I said. "I really appreciate it." I started to walk past her up the stairs, and she touched my leg.

"Sit down," she said. "I don't want to wake Mom and Dad with our yelling."

"We aren't yelling."

"I'm just anticipating," Evelyn said. "So aren't you going to ask what I expect from you? Having been so kind and all?"

"Wait. By 'being so kind,' do you mean snooping around my—"

"I mean cleaning up your mess. I mean making your bed. You're not gonna ask what I expect? I'll tell you anyway. I expect you to tell me what the fuck is going on. Where were you?"

"I can't tell you."

"You *can't* tell me?"

"Okay. I don't want to tell you."

Evelyn stared at me. "Lauren, I know you wouldn't deliberately narc on me, but Sasha . . ."

"This has nothing to do with you," I said. Which was mostly true. It definitely had nothing to do with her in the way she thought it did. And if I told her the truth, I didn't trust her ability to control herself. She'd tell Peter, or she'd post a furious comment to some activist blog the Department keeps under surveillance. (Sasha claims that every activist blog is read by twice as many Department employees as actual "activists.") "And I will never tell Sasha anything about you."

"So you *were* with Sasha."

"I was," I said, realizing I needed to tell Evelyn something or she wouldn't leave it alone. "We were fooling around. That's all."

Her top lip curled. "You were fooling around?"

"I knew you wouldn't approve."

"You're fooling around with a guy who puts people in jail for saying things against the Department." She stared at me. "Why wouldn't I approve of that?"

I stood. The best thing I could do for Evelyn was to let her write me off. That way, when the Department took me in, she wouldn't be tempted to do anything stupid. "The Department keeps people safe. You included. Talking trash about the Department doesn't make you a hero, Ev."

"I don't . . ." She was blinking her eyes more than usual and her voice had a tiny quaver. "I never said I was a hero. I know Peter's been kind of a jerk, but I can't believe you're really buying into the Department's—"

"Believe it. Leave me alone." I walked up the stairs, not wanting her to see my own eyes tearing.

I found my room warm, the window closed. I lay on the fresh sheets Evelyn had put on my bed. After a few minutes I heard Evelyn go into her room. I lay awake for a long time, then eventually got up and typed this into the computer.

I wonder how much time I have left.

Your patient/drug

factory,

Lauren Fielding

JOURNAL OF
LAUREN C. FIELDING

Monday, November 3, 2031

Dr. Corbin:

After everything that happened this weekend, it's weird how *normal* everything feels at school. Riley and Gabriella and I are back to being good friends. Don't get me wrong—it's not like it used to be. I'm not that person anymore. But after the party Saturday night, they seem to have made their peace with the new me. Or maybe I've made my peace with the old them.

Whatever, it is, it feels good to be friends again. I saw Riley at her locker this morning and I stopped. "Hey, Riley!" I said. "Great party!"

She looked surprised for a second, then grinned. "It was pretty great, wasn't it? Sorry you had to leave early. I was so mad about that dirtbag breaking Sasha's glasses. I swear to God, it's the last time I let other people's security into one of my parties." She hesitated. "Someone said *you* beat the guy up afterward."

"Me?" I forced a giggle. "I just pushed between him and Sasha, that's all."

"Well, sorry again."

"Don't worry about it," I said. I stared at her face, looking for a sign of whether or not her father had found out about Sasha and me accessing the Department's system from his office. "How's your dad?"

She gave me an odd look. "I don't know. How's *your* dad?"

I laughed a little. "No, seriously. Is everything okay with him at work?"

Her lips thinned. "Are you joining the Evelyn Fielding school of 'Riley's dad is horrible because he's high up in the Department'?"

"Not at all. It's just I've heard things are a little rocky at the Department, what with the Emergency Act expiring. I was wondering if that's made a difference to your father."

Riley relaxed a little. "As though I would know. I stopped asking my dad about work years ago. I got tired of him making the same stupid joke. 'Hey, Cedar, we'd tell her, but then we'd have to kill her, isn't that right, Cedar? Hey, Cedar, do we tell Riley about work? No! We don't do that.'"

It was a good enough imitation of her father that I found myself laughing. Together, we started walking to first-period chemistry class. "So he hasn't been particularly stressed out or anything lately?"

She snorted. "My dad's never been, like, the most relaxed guy in the world, but I haven't noticed any change."

Evelyn rounded the corner in front of us, and Riley and I automatically paused. Evelyn swept past, not looking at me.

"Whoa. What's up with her?" Riley asked.

I couldn't think of a reason not to tell Riley. "She's mad that I'm dating Sasha."

"She's jealous?"

"No."

"Oh. Right. She's mad because he supposedly works for the Department."

I shot Riley a disbelieving look. "C'mon. Of course he works for the Department. Just ask your dad if you don't believe me."

She held up her hands. "Actually, I have asked my dad. He claims he has no idea. He might even be telling the truth. The Department's a big place. Anyway, what does Evelyn care? Your *father* does contracts for the Department all the time."

I didn't answer Riley, but stared after Evelyn, resisting the urge to chase her down the hallway and apologize. Tell her everything, if that's what it would take for her to not be mad at me. I'm sure she's never been this angry with me before. I actually don't remember her *ever* being mad at me, but that's probably just because I missed it, back when I missed everything.

I didn't see Evelyn again at school, but after school, when Sasha and I were walking home, I saw her walking a block or so ahead of us. Sasha must have noticed the expression on my face because he pointed at me, then at Evelyn, and made a little walking gesture with his index finger and middle finger, obviously inviting me to walk home with my sister. It's amazing how good he is at communicating in ways that his glasses don't catch.

I gave my head a minute shake. The thing is, when you're alienating someone for their own good, you can't tell them, *Hey, I'm alienating you for your own good, so you don't do something stupid and self-sacrificing when the Department picks me up.*

Sasha and I talked about it at the tree house later.

"You want me to talk to your sister?" he said. He'd brought a couple of sleeping bags to the tree house to make it more comfortable, and at this point we were lying together, my head on his shoulder, his arm around me. "It's obviously bothering you, having her furious with you."

I pulled a few inches away and eyed him incredulously. "You think *you* talking to her would help?"

"I don't mean give her a hard time about her politics. I mean appeal to her bleeding heart. Let her know my refugee background. I can be really pathetic." He widened his eyes and blinked.

I snorted. "That doesn't look pathetic. It looks like you have something in your eye."

"That could be pathetic." He clapped his free hand over his right eye, and said, "Argh. My eye. I . . . I think I'm blind now. Damn it. That was my favorite eye, too. Now I can never become a champion archer."

I laughed again, but quickly sobered. "I don't want Evelyn to feel sorry for you. I want her to write me off. Corbin's going to bring me in at some point, and when she does, I want Evelyn to think something like 'Well, too bad, but she brought that on herself, running around with a Departmental agent.' "

He eyed me skeptically. "You think that's going to work? She's not an idiot. You and I could also just stay away from each other during the day. Evelyn wouldn't be nearly so mad at you if she didn't see the two of us hanging out all the time. And it's not like you and I can really talk while I'm wearing my glasses anyway."

"Sure we can talk." I put my head back on his shoulder. "Just not about the Department or my origins as a laboratory rat. Not my favorite topics of conversation anyway. I don't want to stop walking home with you." I suppose I could pretend this is a rational thing. Like I'm worried about getting taken in earlier if I stop hanging out with Sasha. But the truth is, I just don't want to stay away from him.

He's the one person who knows what I am. Why I was created. And he still likes me. I know he's a liar, and a Departmental agent who's also working with some third party. I know I can't trust him, and I don't. But he's funny and kind and he knows what I am, and he still likes me. That much is true and not a lie. I feel it when he touches me.

My time with him today was the best part of my day. The one part when—for a few minutes, anyway—I felt like I could just be myself.

JOURNAL OF
LAUREN C. FIELDING

Wednesday, November 5, 2031

Dr. Corbin:

I got your messages yesterday and the day before. You're
starting to lose patience with me, aren't you? You know what's
weird? I'm *almost* tempted to start sending you my real journal
entries again. Not that I trust you, or that I'm getting stupid
again.

But I feel like I'm going crazy, and you probably *are* one of the
only people in the world who would understand. Mostly because
it's your fault.

I feel like my brain is splitting in two. I think most people figure out early how to dissemble—how to show other people just a
part of what they're thinking and feeling. I never had to learn that,

and now I have this inside-self and this outside-self, and they're getting further and further apart.

On the one hand, I've been walking around with this pit of anger in my stomach all week. Just looking for a fight. Today I walked out of English class and I happened to see Jimmy Porten down the hall. I don't know what he saw in my face, but he turned on his heel and ran in the opposite direction. And it was the smart thing for him to do, too. I was totally ready—not just ready, but eager, crazily eager—to kick his ass, to hurt him, to make him feel some piece of what I'm feeling.

At self-defense class yesterday evening, I almost broke Nora Edgemont's arm. Nora Edgemont, for God's sake. The most clean-cut, straight-A, volunteers-for-the-canned-food-drive-around-Christmas-and-volunteers-in-the-animal-shelter-the-rest-of-the-time person you've ever met. She even smells pure. Like baby kittens or something.

We matched up to spar last night. We used to be great sparring partners, in part because she was the only person in class who was nearly as bad as I was.

Last night we started like we always used to. She smiled at me. I smiled at her. "You ready?" she said.

"Any time!" I said, still smiling, even as my stomach churned acid up the back of my throat, even as I wondered: When are they going to come for me? Tonight? Tomorrow? What does Dr. Corbin even want with me now that she's taken the Innocence Treatment from my brain?

Nora started with a right overhand jab. Not hard. Not—and I want to emphasize this—not in any way mean-spirited or underhanded. I ducked the jab easily, grabbed her arm, kicked her legs out from under her, and took her down.

And here's where it almost got crazy. Her left arm was pinned beneath her and I had her right arm wrapped up in an armlock. She couldn't tap out. And for a second, I had the thought: *I could break her arm and I'd just say, "She didn't tap out. I didn't know I was hurting her, not in time."* No one would blame me.

I was lying on top of her, the clean soapy smell of her mingling with the smell of old sweat and rubber coming off the mat, and I could clearly imagine the sound of the crack, the sound of her scream. I cranked her elbow another millimeter or two, and she gasped. At that last moment, I let her go. Rolled off her, and helped her to her feet. Massaged her elbow a little bit to make sure it was okay.

"Sorry," I said.

"Why?" She looked puzzled. "You didn't hurt me."

"Oh. Good." I forced a smile so fake it hurt my cheeks.

"You've gotten really good, Lauren. Have you been practicing?"

"A little," I said. "Yeah."

"You want to go again?" she said. "I won't go so easy on you this time!"

I shook my head, smile still plastered on my face. "I think I'll sit down for a few minutes."

I waited until Nora was sparring with someone else and then I found one of the teaching assistants free. A big, hulking guy called

194

Lukas who always hits a little too hard, who I probably couldn't hurt even if I tried. And for a few blessed minutes I fought with him and didn't think about anything at all.

So there's all this anger simmering inside me. That would make me feel crazy enough. But there's also the nice, old-Lauren side of me. The person who apologized to Nora. The one who let Jimmy run off and made herself stop glaring after him. The one who's back to being good friends with Riley and Gabriella. Just a regular girl at Allegheny High School.

Aside from Evelyn not wanting to have anything to do with me (my dad had to drive me to Benitez's class last night, as Evelyn refused to go), there's almost no sign of how different I am. I'm at the same school, with the same locker I've had for the last two and a half years, hanging out with the same friends I've had for a decade. Everything in my life (aside from the back of my head) looks pretty much the same as it did last year. But I'm walking around feeling like I'm a tourist in my own life. How can I feel nostalgic for a life that I'm still living?

If I thought you could answer that, Dr. Corbin, I'd be much more likely to call you back. Speaking of which, Sasha keeps telling me I need to stay in touch with you. He thinks if I keep writing fake journal entries and agreeing to come in for regular checkups, you won't feel the need to pull me in.[18]

---

[18] Around this time I remember our father telling Lauren she *had* to go see Dr. Corbin. It was perhaps the first time in Lauren's life that she outright refused to do what our father told her. I remember how baffled he was. As an aside: it's interesting how little Lauren talks about our parents

195

But honestly, Dr. Corbin, you and I both know you're not going to leave me alone. I saw the way you looked at me last time I came in; I heard the tone of your voice on my voice mail today and yesterday and the day before yesterday. There's no way you're going to let me walk away.

So screw you. Leave all the messages you want. If you want me, you're going to have to convince the Department to arrest a sixteen-year-old girl with a mental disability who's never said a word against the Department. I'm sure you can do it. I just hope it's a real pain in the ass.

---

in her journal entries. She was extremely close to our father, especially, and I can't help but think his absence in her journal was a deliberate effort on her part to direct attention away from our family.

CASE NOTES OF DR. FINLAY BRECHEL

December 11, 2031

Transcribed from interview:

What's wrong, Dr. Brechel?

Nothing's wrong. How are you feeling this morning?

Disturbed by my therapist. You're fidgeting much more than you usually do, and I've never seen you so distracted by the surveillance cameras. Has Paxeon threatened you?

No one's threatened me.

So why are you so upset?

I'm not so upset.

(long silence)

Lauren. Part of being in a therapeutic relationship

is that the therapist doesn't—can't—share
everything with their patient. It wouldn't be
good for you, and it would make it very difficult
for me to maintain the appropriate distance. So
while there may be something bothering me,
perhaps the better question for us to explore is,
why should that matter to you?

Dr. Brechel, you're the one person I see all day
who's not an orderly putting me in handcuffs or
delivering food. So of course it matters to me.

(pause)

They didn't threaten you, but there's definitely
something . . . Have they extended the Emergency
Act? It's something about the Emergency Act,
isn't it? Dr. Brechel, did they extend it or not?

Not yet. They—I—Lauren, I have to insist. This
therapy is about you, not about me. Not about
the United States' government.

Dr. Brechel, I don't need therapy. I need to get out
of here.

Let's talk about that feeling, that sense of being
here against your will. You've mentioned that
many times in our sessions and yet I've seen the
documents you signed when you came in. You
voluntarily committed yourself.

I guess. I mean, in the sense that everything is
voluntary in some way. Like you working for

Paxeon, right? You might not like it, but you'd rather eat than not eat. You'd rather wear that nice watch than not wear that nice watch.

Are you saying they paid you to commit yourself to Paxeon's custody?

In a way, I guess they did. You should really just download my journal.

Right. (voice rising) I should download files from a website classified as "terrorist." I'm working in a goddamn Paxeon facility, using the network provided to Paxeon by the goddamn Dep—

Dr. Brechel!

(hoarse breathing)

You should calm down. You almost said something you would have regretted.

I'm sorry, Lauren. I . . . I'm . . . This is a stressful time for me. Let me ask again: why did you commit yourself to Paxeon's custody? Please don't tell me to download your—

The Department arrested Evelyn.

What?

You heard me. The Department arrested Evelyn. I made a deal with Dr. Corbin to get her out. Guess what it was.

JOURNAL OF
LAUREN C. FIELDING

Sunday, November 9, 2031

Dear Dr. Corbin,

I'm editing this from the car as my parents drive me to the airport. I have about an hour left of freedom, maybe in my whole life. I wonder what my parents think I'm writing. One more journal entry to the benevolent Dr. Corbin? Ha. That would be a good title if I turned my journal entries into a book. *The Benevolent Dr. Corbin.* It has a nice ring to it, don't you think?

As soon as I finish writing this entry I'm going to upload it . . . upload all my real journal entries to a few of the pirate websites and schedule them to go live on December 4—one month before the Emergency Act expires. Hopefully people will read them. Hopefully it will make a difference.

The Department arrested Evelyn on Friday.

I walked into the lunchroom and Gabriella ran up to me. "I'm so sorry, Lauren!"

"For what?" I said. But I already knew. Something in the way she said it, the way that the people around were watching me. The fact that I couldn't see Evelyn anywhere, and if there was something for Gabriella to be sorry about, Evelyn should have been right there, being sorry, too, no matter how furious she was with me.

"I just heard," Gabriella said. "Vince Alvarez was at his locker when the police went past. They took Evelyn out of AP Calculus in handcuffs."

"In handcuffs?" I said. I felt cold all over, super-aware, like the moment before Jimmy Porten had lunged at me. They'd taken Evelyn out of school in handcuffs. That meant no quick release where she could deny ever having been arrested. They might never release her, and even if they did, her life in the United States was ruined.

I scanned the lunchroom. There. I ran toward Sasha. His smile quickly disappeared when he saw the look on my face. "What?" he said. "What is it?"

I snatched the glasses from his face and flicked them as hard as I could across the room. "Who paid you to delete those files they had on me?" I hissed.

He licked his lips and shook his head. "It's not safe for me to tell you."

"This from the guy who helped me break into the Department's network? Was that safe?" I kept my voice low, but Sasha shifted nervously.

"What is it?" he said. "What happened?"

"They publicly arrested Evelyn."

"Oh shit. I'm so sorry."

I'd swear he was genuinely sorry, not that it really mattered.

"You know they just arrested her to get you."

"Yeah," I said. "I know. Well, it worked. I'm going to call Corbin right now."

"Don't do it. They'll just arrest Evelyn again whenever they feel like it."

"I'll make sure she's out of the country before I go in."

"Before you go in and what? Sign yourself over to Paxeon?"

"Whatever they want." I hesitated. I still didn't know what Corbin wanted with me. Something to do with her research, but what? "Commit myself to their custody, I'm guessing. Let Corbin run whatever experiment she wants on me."

He shook his head. "Don't do it," he said again. "They'll never let you go."

"Maybe. Which would make this your last chance to tell me: who paid you to delete my files?"

He shook his head again. "I can't, Lauren . . . There's drugs they'll give you—the Department has these drugs—you won't be able to keep secrets no matter how hard you try."

"You'd know, wouldn't you?" I said.

He met my eyes. "Yeah. I would."

We stared at each other for a few more seconds. I swear I don't understand myself. Even then, my world falling apart around me,

I simultaneously wanted him dead and just . . . wanted him. That can't be normal.

"I'm posting my journals," I told him. "The real journals."

His eyes widened. "Your real journals? Lauren, if the Department finds out that I helped you break into their system—"

"I'll set it to go live in December," I said. "December 4. That gives you almost four weeks to figure something out." He started to say something, and I interrupted. "I'm not keeping Paxeon's secrets for them, Sasha, and if I don't post it now, I won't get another chance." I made myself meet his eyes. "Goodbye."

"Lauren—" His voice faltered.

I waited for the handful of seconds it took him to realize there was nothing else to say. Then I turned and left. He didn't call after me.

By the way, if you're reading this, Sasha—and I hope you do read this someday—I picture you downloading and reading it while you eat your macaroni and cheese dinner in whatever empty house they have you living in next and . . . my God, now I'm feeling sorry for *you*. I'm still such an idiot.

Anyway.

If you're reading this, Sasha, I really wish you could tell me: did we ever have anything real?

Doesn't seem likely, does it? You having the chance to tell me anything, I mean. My parents and I just passed the first sign for the airport. Thirty-one miles to go.

Dr. Corbin, you made a mistake when you had Evelyn arrested.

Once you showed me that I couldn't protect my family, well . . . I have nothing to lose. I don't mean that in a melodramatic way. Just purely factual. There's no reason for me to keep your secrets if keeping them isn't going to protect the people I love.

On the contrary. If I'm in Paxeon's custody, and if everyone knows about the Innocence Treatment, the Department will have no reason to come after my family. My family won't know anything more than anyone else. I'm guessing the Department will dismiss my posts as the ravings of a crazy person (though I presume they'll have some fancier way of saying "crazy,")[19] and they won't want to bring anyone else's attention to them by, say, detaining my whole family. Shoot—if the Emergency Act doesn't get reauthorized, they might actually have to start giving reasons before they can detain people.

Point is, after I said goodbye to Sasha I walked out of the cafeteria and called you. There was no point in wasting time. Not with Evelyn on her way to prison.

A receptionist picked up. "Good morning! Paxeon," she said sweetly. "How may I direct your call?"

"Could you connect me to Dr. Patricia Corbin, please?"

"Who shall I say is calling?"

"Lauren Fielding."

---

[19] In fact, in December 2031, a Department spokesperson described Lauren's just-posted journal entries as the "completely unfounded allegations of a young woman with a well-documented and tragic history of cognitive and mental disability." (*nytimes.com,* Monday, December 8, 2031.)

"Is she expecting your call?"

I surprised myself by laughing. A sense of humor has got to be my favorite part of my postoperation brain. "Definitely. Yes she is."

"One moment please, Ms. Fielding."

An instant of elevator music, and then I heard your voice, silky and serene. "Hello?"

"Let her go, and I'll come in," I said.

Credit where credit's due, Dr. Corbin. You didn't pretend to misunderstand me. "Lauren," you said. "Nice to hear from you, dear. I heard about your sister's arrest and I believe I *could* get her free. Of course, I'll have to ask that you commit yourself to our care first."

I laughed again. This time the laughter hurt my throat, clenched tight with tension. "And I'll have to ask that you go fuck yourself. Get her out first. If I don't turn myself in, you can always get her arrested again."

"I don't think that would work for us, dear. How about you come in at the same time that the Department releases Evelyn? The Department has some experience in prisoner swaps. Not that you'll be a prisoner of the Department, you understand, but we could use that synchronous framework to assuage both of our concerns."

"I'll come in the day after Evelyn is released. I want to say goodbye to Evelyn and put my family on a flight out of the country. Then I'll come in."

"Do you think they'll go without you, dear?" You sounded genuinely curious. "They seem very attached. In any case, I can't give you an entire day. What if you change your mind? What if you decide to put yourself on that same airplane out of the country?"

"Fine. Let's do the exchange at the airport," I said. "When my family is all on the plane, I'll walk off and hand myself over. If I don't, you can have us all pulled off the flight and arrested."

"I don't *want* to have you arrested," you said, a little less gently. "For God's sake, I've been bending over backward to avoid placing you in the Department's custody."

You paused, and I could hear your breath slow, could imagine you counting down from ten as you calmed yourself. When you spoke again, your voice was composed. "But I take your point. An airport exchange should be fine. That said, are you *sure* you want your family out of the country? Don't you want them close by where they can visit you? Where they can pick you up when we release you in a few weeks? I don't think your treatment will take all that long."

I sighed. The hardest lies to catch are the ones that you want to believe. But I wasn't a sucker anymore. "Just have the tickets and Evelyn waiting at the airport. Text me the flight information, and we'll be there. Once I see their flight take off—and I want tickets on a commercial airline, nothing military or Department controlled—once I see their flight take off, I'll come quietly." I hung up.

I stared at my phone for a few seconds, not believing how easy it had been to bargain away my freedom. Not believing I was actually going to do it. Except of course I am. What choice do I have?

I'm going to upload all of this now. I don't know if anyone will ever read it. If they do, I don't know if it will do any good. I'd like to believe it will shift things enough that Congress won't dare to renew the Emergency Act. But I'd like to believe in unicorns, too, and they don't seem too damn likely.

I should probably try to end on a more uplifting, inspirational note, but my dad just took the airport exit. If I don't upload this now, I never will.

Sincerely yours,

Lauren Cathleen Fielding

EDITOR'S NOTE: INTERLUDE

Reluctant as I am to insert my own perspective into Lauren's narrative, there are some gaps here in Lauren's journal entries that I feel obliged to fill.

It may be hard to remember how terrifying the Innocence Treatment was when it emerged a decade ago. People's last refuge—their own thoughts and beliefs—were suddenly not their own.

The terror of that is what made Lauren so famous—along with the related gratitude. Bad as it was to learn about the Innocence Treatment, it would have been far worse if we hadn't known about it. Friends would have betrayed friends . . . spouses would have betrayed spouses . . . and no one would have understood why. Not the betrayed, and not the betrayer. Imagine sleeping with another man, and not knowing why you had betrayed your husband. Trying to explain to your husband—and yourself—that you had loved the other man so much at that moment, that it had seemed impossible to say no.

For me, the memory of the period immediately following Lauren's revelations is tangled up with my own personal terror after spending two days in the Department's "administrative detention." I'm not sure what made those two days so frightening. No one tortured me. No one even questioned me. They locked me in a windowless cell with a woman who had been there for three months without seeing a lawyer, without having a visit from her family. Without seeing anyone at all, except for the guards who brought her food.

Three months may not seem like a long time, but it had been more than long enough to drive that poor woman around the bend. She had a few lucid moments, but mostly she lay on her bed and cried. Sometimes a low, moaning sob, sometimes full-scale weeping. I never found out what she was in for. I'm not sure she even knew.

After two days and two nights, a guard came to fetch me. "Good news," she told me cheerily, ignoring my sobbing cell mate. "You're being released."

She handcuffed me and led me down the hall. I didn't look back at my cell mate. To be honest, I didn't think of her again for weeks. That's how selfless I turned out to be. Not much of an idealist when my own safety was on the line.

Blinking in the bright winter sunlight, I found one of the Department's infamous black vans waiting for me at the prison entrance.

"Don't worry," the guard who had collected me said. "We're just taking you to the airport. Someone very important has taken an interest in you." She loaded me into the back of the van, still handcuffed, and got in the front seat with the driver. The bench seats in back were hard plastic and smelled strongly of bleach with a slight undertone of vomit. I sat in the back, alone, staring at the blank walls of the van, wondering where they were really taking me.

You can't imagine how surprised I was when they pulled over a few hours later and slid open the van's back door, and I found myself facing a large INTERNATIONAL DEPARTURES sign. Two porters in blue uniforms smoked by the curbside check-in booth, and a woman walked by pushing a stroller with one hand and pulling a small suitcase after her with the other. The airport. They'd actually taken me to the airport.

A few seconds later an airport security guy arrived to meet my guards. Together, they escorted me past the airlines' check-in desks and through security, bypassing the metal detectors and X-ray machines and heading straight toward the gates. Crowds of people waiting at security watched as I was led past them in handcuffs.

We stopped in front of gate C12. The electronic display said: BA 312 TO HEATHROW. NOW BOARDING.

One of the guards unlocked my handcuffs. The other guard handed me some papers, which turned out to be an airplane ticket and a provisional visa for the UK. "Safe travels, Ms. Fielding," she said. She almost smiled at the look on my face. Not quite.

I ran onto the airplane, expecting at any moment to be stopped. The flight attendants took my ticket and waved me on, for all the world like I was just another passenger. I found Lauren and my parents waiting for me in coach class. There were no empty seats around them.

Lauren quickly stood. "Evelyn," she said. She had tears in her eyes, and I remember thinking it was the first time I'd seen her cry since just after her operation.

"Lauren."

We hugged. She put her lips next to my ear and whispered, "Keep Mom and Dad on the plane. Don't let them make a fuss. Make sure I'm not doing this for nothing."

"Doing what?" I pulled away from her.

Louder, so our parents could hear, she said, "Take my seat, Ev. I'll get the attendant to assign us another seat." She winked at our dad. "Maybe they'll let me stay in first class."

She walked past me, not giving our parents a second look. Nothing to let them know what she was doing. I discovered later that she'd told them a story about how Dr. Corbin was happy to help, how the Department really didn't want to keep me, but just needed a way of saving face, so we were all going to the UK for a few months. God knows how she convinced them, but Lauren was an extremely good liar by then. And they were desperate to believe her, I'm sure—desperate to believe that I'd be released from jail without any lasting damage to me or them.

A minute or two after Lauren walked away, the plane started taxiing for takeoff. My parents assumed Lauren had been given a seat up front. By the time they realized the truth, it was too late—we were an hour over the Atlantic. My parents had a choice: they could throw a fit, possibly forcing the plane to turn around and land, at which point we'd all be arrested, or they could let Lauren's sacrifice mean something.

They never made their peace with it, though. My dad spent weeks trying every contact he had in the Department. People stopped taking his calls, but he didn't stop calling.

In the end, my parents surprised everyone—including themselves—by becoming anti-Department activists. To date, they have never returned to the U.S. They sold their house in Maryland later that year and bought a tiny apartment in the Willesden neighborhood of London. Willesden was just in the process of becoming London's Little New York, filled with American dissidents and refugees of every stripe imaginable. These days you can walk around Willesden for hours without hearing a British accent— that's how many expatriated Americans have settled there.

My parents used the rest of the money from the sale of their house to fund Innocence.org—a nonprofit providing resources and information to victims or potential victims of the Innocence Treatment. If you go to their website, you'll find the latest news of successful treatments and the latest (debunked) rumors of vaccines that can make you immune to the Innocence Treatment.

Ironically, I was the one—teenaged activist and wonder child—I was the one who rejected activism. My high school sent me my diploma and I started university in Spain a few months later. I buried myself in the study of twentieth-century Chinese literature, becoming fluent in Mandarin and Cantonese, with every intention of losing myself in the Chinese academy.

I had no intention of editing a book like this. For years, I wouldn't admit to any connection with Lauren—that's how terrified I was of drawing the attention of the Department. I started going by my middle name. People would ask if I was related to the Innocence Girl, and I'd laugh. I practiced the laugh until it sounded real, though no doubt Lauren would have seen through it in an instant. "Ha. No. I get that all the time. Fielding is such a common name."

I couldn't help hearing rumors about Lauren from time to time. I hoped the good ones were true and prayed the bad ones were not. I tried to believe that I could put it all behind me. Live whatever passed for a normal life in the twenty-first century.

But enough about me. What follows are five never-before-published entries from Lauren's journal *after* she went into Paxeon's custody. A panel of independent forensic-document examiners has verified that these journal entries were written by my sister during the period in question. I've posted the verification documents online at Innocence.org, and filed the originals with my aggregator.

Thank you for your continued interest.

Dr. E. Sofia Fielding, Ph.D.
London, UK
June 2041

FROM THE PRISON JOURNAL
OF LAUREN C. FIELDING

December 9, 2031

Funny how attached I've gotten to keeping a journal, even one that no one else will ever read. I'm scribbling this on a notebook I begged from my therapist, writing in the bathroom (where I'm pretty sure there's no security camera) with the lights out (just in case). Though, clearly, if Dr. Corbin really wanted to read it, I'm in no position to stop her.

I couldn't quite bring myself to keep addressing my journal to Dr. Corbin when just writing her name makes me want to ram my fist down her throat. (How's that for a violent and paranoid thought, Dr. Brechel?)

Poor Dr. Brechel. Still trying to convince himself that I'm crazy. As long as he believes I'm crazy, he doesn't have to accept how deeply screwed he is.

Kind of funny, kind of sad: Dr. Brechel has a new watch that I'm almost sure he bought with the advance he got from Paxeon. It's made of some expensive silvery alloy, and I know it's new because it doesn't match the tan line on his wrist. He touches it every time I tell him he should run. I think it reassures him. He didn't throw away his life for nothing—he got a really fancy watch out of it.

Not that I'm complaining. I'm glad he took the job. Dr. Brechel is a good person, especially as far as Paxeon employees go. He has them take off my restraints when he and I meet, and he gave me the pad and pencil I'm writing with right now. The pencil is kept blunt in case I get the urge to stab someone with it, but at least it writes. Locked up in a windowless cell twenty hours a day, it makes a big difference, having a way to write and sketch and just generally not go any crazier than I already am.

Along those lines, I've given myself a schedule. I wake up, do push-ups, sit-ups, draw, write, push-ups, sit-ups, draw, write, and so on. Eat when they bring me food. Sleep as much as possible. Not nearly as much as I'd like. Work out with the makeshift punching bag I've made in the bathroom. (I've wrapped my towels around the towel bar, which makes an okay punching bag. I don't mind bruising my knuckles a little.) So that's twenty hours a day.

As for the other four hours, I have two hour-long sessions with Dr. Brechel every day, and then there's my gym time. They've converted one of the offices on this floor into a mini-gym—a treadmill, some weights, and a real punching bag. I think it's like giving a guinea pig a wheel to run on. Dr. Corbin doesn't want ill health interfering with the results of her latest tests. Still, I can't resist. They turn me loose in the gym twice a day and I make the most of it.

Speaking of tests, they've given me an injection or two every day that I've been here. Plus a nasal spray the first day I arrived. At first I was worried—terrified, really—that they were going to turn me back into an idiot. But so far that hasn't happened. Whatever they've given me, I still don't believe anything these liars tell me. I still have no problem telling when Dr. Brechel is trying to keep something from me. There was the one day last week when I thought Dr. Brechel was the funniest man I'd ever met, but whatever that was wore off pretty quickly.

Even then, the drugs didn't *make* me talk to him. I could have kept my mouth shut if I wanted. I probably should have kept my mouth shut, if I cared as much about Brechel surviving this job as I pretend to. But it feels good to be honest with someone—like writing this journal, I guess. After the first session or two with Dr. Brechel, I stopped trying to resist.

Plus, if he listens to me about setting up a webpage to be published in the event of his death, that's one more piece of evidence out there in the world. Which, by the way, is why I didn't tell him what happened between me and Eric Schafer. I imagined Mom and Dad reading Dr. Brechel's account and . . . well, yuck. Some things they don't have to know.

What happened was this: I'd just come into Paxeon custody when I saw him again. Eric Schafer—the orderly I remembered being so nice. I wasn't restrained yet.

216

Some other orderly was leading me up to my new room. This place has become a ghost town compared to how it used to be when I visited with my parents. Paxeon headquarters used to *bustle*. Tons of scientists wandering around, chatting or hunched over their tablets. People in expensive suits striding down the hallway carrying briefcases.

All of that's gone. The day I came in, the lobby was empty except for the orderly who was waiting for me. We took the elevator to the seventh floor and found the hallway empty, too, except for Schafer.

"Lauren!" Schafer said, coming toward me, both arms out for a hug. He's a short, broad man, balding with a few tufts of blond hair on either side of his head. The orderly who had brought me walked past Schafer, headed for a computer terminal at the other end of the hall.

"I heard you were coming back." Schafer smiled, arms still outstretched. His eyes flicked down to my chest and stayed there. "So nice to see you again. I'm really looking forward to your stay!"

I stared at him, hazy memories surfacing from when I'd been heavily sedated after the operation. Eric touching me. Eric bathing me. The smug smile on his face as he soaped up my breasts. "Stay away from me," I said, stepping back toward the elevator.

Eric's forehead creased. "Shoot," he said. "We got along so well on your last visit." He folded his arms, muscular and pale, across his chest and smiled at me. That same smug smile.

I stopped retreating. "You're not going to be my orderly this time."

Eric's eyes strayed to the camera mounted on the wall. "Sorry, Lauren, but that's not my decision or yours." He walked toward me. "I'll show you to your room."

"Make it your decision," I said, trying to control my anger. "Stay away from me. Quit if you have to. I don't want to see you again."

"I'm sure we're going to get along fine, once you get settled—"

"No," I said. "You're not going to get along fine. Not anymore."

I drove my knee between his legs. One thing I've realized since the operation is that *wanting* to hurt someone else is more dangerous than any martial-art technique. Just being willing to inflict pain without any warning. Most people aren't. Not without a drink or working themselves up into self-righteous anger. Not without hesitating for a few seconds between blows.

He doubled over and gasped. I didn't hesitate.

I grabbed his hair and stepped behind him, pulling him off balance, then kneed him hard in the throat as he went down. He curled up on the floor and I stamped the heel of my boot down on his right hand. He made a kind of strangled squeal, in too much pain to scream.

I leaned over him and whispered, "I want you to quit. Today. Get a job where I never have to see you again. Nod to show you understand."

"Bitch," he managed to gasp. "Can't . . . wait . . . till . . . they . . . fix . . . you back."

That's when I broke his leg. I kicked the side of his thigh, just above his knee. It's a kick I've practiced hundreds of times at self-defense class. I put just as much force into it as I did when I broke

218

three boards in last spring's exhibition. I heard his leg crack and he screamed.

I leaned back over him. "If I see you again, I'll kill you. I'll kill you, and I'll walk away laughing. Nod to show you understand."

Tears were running down his face. He nodded.

The whole thing had taken maybe thirty seconds. The other orderly had run back to us and was staring at me, eyes wide, so scared I could see the pulse in his neck.

"Make sure the other orderlies hear about this," I said. "Make sure they know that I hold grudges."

He nodded, swallowing heavily and staring at Eric, who had passed out on the floor.

That was pretty much the most fun I've had since being committed. The only fun. I just wish it had been Dr. Corbin instead. She hasn't let me see her since I got here. My guess is she's worried about me figuring out what she has planned for me. Not because she cares about my feelings, you understand, but because it might throw off the results of her experiment if I know too much about it.

Nothing else to write for now. Off to do push-ups, punch the towel rack, and stare at the wall until lunch arrives.

FROM THE PRISON JOURNAL OF LAUREN C. FIELDING

December 12, 2031

This morning Dr. Brechel told me the Emergency Act won't be renewed. I smiled, and he had the gall to tell me not to celebrate too soon. As though I was the sucker who had let Paxeon bribe me into its clutches for the price of a nice watch.

"You still didn't download my journals, did you?" I asked.

"No," he said. "But now maybe—"

"Don't do it now," I said.

He looked up at the video cameras.

"No, I'm not just saying this for the cameras. I'm saying it because now is the last time you want to get the Department's attention. All due respect, but you've been an idiot, and now you're screwed. Not quite as much as I am, but still."

He frowned, not understanding. Or not wanting to understand.

"If the act isn't renewed, the folks in the Department could be prosecuted for the stuff they've done over the last ten years. You and I are already seeming like inconvenient leftovers to someone. Leftovers with embarrassing, even dangerous, stories to tell."

He didn't say anything then. Didn't ask me anything, either, just sat there staring, this scared and stupid look in his eyes. I've never been to a slaughterhouse, but I imagine it's the same look a cow would have as it approaches the slaughterhouse floor on the conveyor belt, the smell of blood getting too strong for it to ignore.

"Dr. Brechel," I said. "You know how I told you to quit before you got in too deep?"

He nodded dumbly. "Yes. I should quit—"

"No. Too late. Your best bet now is to keep your head down. Keep to your usual schedule. Keep filing reports about me. Don't get anyone's attention. They let you out of here sometimes, don't they?"

"Of course they let me out of here," he said, his voice thick and slow. It gathered energy, became a bit more normal as he continued. "I'm not a prisoner, Lauren."

"Great. Lucky you. So don't quit. Go to a movie. Better, take a weekend off to . . . I don't know, visit your kids or watch snow fall in New England. Whatever. The point is, don't quit. Just leave and don't come back. Call in sick for a few days. Get out of the country and wait for things to settle down. The Department is scared, Dr. Brechel. Scared people do stupid things. But if the Emergency Act isn't renewed—" I let the smile creep back onto my face. The Emergency Act wasn't going be renewed. At least my death would mean something. "They're gonna have other things to worry about. Don't get their attention, and you'll be fine."

He nodded to himself, lips pursed, tapping his stylus on the edge of his tablet. Finally he said, "What makes you such an expert on the world, Lauren?" There was an edge I hadn't heard in his voice before. Hostility. Active dislike, even. "You get an operation that takes off some blinkers, makes you more observant, okay. But why would that make you any better than me at gauging how the Department is going to react to all this?"

I don't think he was expecting an answer, but the truth seemed obvious.

"You hope too much," I said. "You're so busy hoping that you're not paying attention to what's really happening."

"Ah shit." The hostility left Brechel's face as quickly as it had swept over it, leaving only defeat. "Could be. You know who *did* download your journal?"

"Who?"

"Half the Senate. Maybe more. Senator Witherspoon of Colorado was waving your picture around on the Senate floor yesterday. You're famous, Lauren. The press is calling you the Innocence Girl."

I thought I was resigned to death. From the moment I posted my journal entries and committed myself to Paxeon custody, what else could I expect? Still, when he told me a U.S. senator had been waving a picture of me around, I felt a thrill of pure fear. The Department couldn't let me live now. Even if Dr. Corbin wanted to keep me alive, the decision was going to be out of her hands soon. If it wasn't already.

I thought about making a break for it right then, but there was nowhere to go. Two orderlies waited outside the locked steel door to Brechel's office, and anyway, there were seven floors between me and escape. At that moment, if the windows hadn't been barred, I might have taken my chance with a seven-story fall instead of waiting for the Department to come and get me. I wish I knew what they're waiting for. Maybe with the Emergency Act not getting renewed, they're worried about being prosecuted. But I doubt it. I'm pretty sure my name is on a list somewhere and it's just a matter of days before they get to me. Once the Emergency Act expires, it's going to be harder to clean up messes like me.

"Anything else you want to talk about today?" Brechel asked, taking some kind of solace in sticking to his script.

I shook my head, not trusting my voice.

He hesitated, then put out his hand.

I stood and took his hand. It was the first time I'd touched another person's skin (in a nonviolent way) since I'd arrived. His hand was moist and trembling slightly.

"I'll see you tomorrow," he said.

"I hope not," I said. "Get out of here. Keep your head down and go."

"Have a good night." He turned away from me as he rang the bell, telling the orderlies to unlock the door. I think he was crying.

I have a bad feeling that he didn't listen to me. That he tried something stupid and dramatic. No one thinks straight when they're scared.

FROM THE PRISON JOURNAL
OF LAUREN C. FIELDING

December 13, 2031

No meetings with Dr. Brechel today. Instead two security guards and two medical orderlies escorted me out of my cell. I recognized the medical orderlies—a Latino man and a Chinese woman. They've been in and out of my room since I came here: delivering meals, taking blood samples, and so on. The security guards were new, though. Big guys, crew cuts, arms the size of a normal person's torso. On loan from the Department, I'm guessing. The walls closing in on me.

All four of them—the guards and orderlies—were wearing Tasers. At first I thought they were guns. When I first saw them—the two big guys at my door, guns holstered at their hips—I figured they were here to kill me. I figured the game was up. The Department was tying up loose ends before the Emergency Act expired.

I didn't bother trying to run. I wasn't cuffed yet, but they were between me and the door. I guess I could have made a break for my bathroom—made it a little harder for them, but I didn't want to be shot in the back. I'm not sure why I cared. I just knew that I wanted to be looking at the person who killed me. I wanted them to see my face when I died. I wanted my blood to get all over them. (And yeah, I know that's a grim little goal.)

So I didn't run. I stood my ground and stared up at them. Despite their thin-lipped glares, they were just a few years older than me. "Are you here to kill me?"

The guy in front didn't pretend to be shocked. He shook his head. "No. We're here to lead you to a room for some tests." He was telling the truth as far as he knew. He pulled the cuffs out of his belt and came toward me.

"Oh come on." I backed away. "There's four of you. You seriously think you need handcuffs?"

He glanced at the other military guy, a little uncomfortable. It struck me that they'd be more comfortable shooting me than wrestling handcuffs and ankle cuffs onto me.

"Not about what I think, Ms. Fielding. We have orders to put you in handcuffs." His tone was almost apologetic. "If you come quietly we can skip the ankle cuffs for now."

I shrugged and held my hands out in front of me. I've found that if I hold my hands out to be cuffed, they'll almost always put the cuffs on in front of me. Otherwise they cuff my hands behind me, which is both less comfortable and more constraining.

The guy who'd been talking came forward and briskly put my handcuffs on. "What's your name?" I asked.

"Jeff," he said, a little startled.

"Last name?"

He didn't answer.

"You worried I'm going to tell on you, Jeff?" I said. "That maybe your family will find out that part of your job is handcuffing sixteen-year-old girls and leading them to be tortured?"

"You're not going to be tortured," he said. He didn't sound nearly as sure as I would have liked.

They led me down two flights of stairs. This was my first time off the seventh floor since I'd committed myself to Paxeon custody. The lower floors weren't secured like my floor—I didn't see any barred windows or steel doors.

A small bud of hope unfolded inside me. I studied the two new security guards carefully. Every few steps, their right hands casually brushed the handles of what I'd taken to be their guns. Around then I got a better look at their weapons and realized they weren't guns. The handles were blockier and had some yellow zigzags on them. Tasers.

They led me to a small boardroom. Gray December sunlight streamed through the windows (unbarred but we were still on the fifth floor). There was a table with comfortable chairs, and a big monitor at one end of the room.

"Please sit down, Ms. Fielding." Jeff directed me to one of the chairs facing the video monitor.

I sat, saying nothing. The others all relaxed a little. The two medical orderlies took up places on either side of my chair. I noticed that the male orderly, standing to my left, had left the holster of his Taser unsnapped. Careless.

Jeff walked around the table and sat in the chair directly across from me. He placed a small bag on the table, unzipped it, and removed an envelope. He looked up at the surveillance camera mounted in a corner of the ceiling. "Commencing experimental protocol five," he said, slowly and clearly. I wondered what the first four experimental protocols had been. Things they'd already done to me? Or things they'd tried on other people?

He turned to me and started reading from a paper attached to the back of the envelope. "Good afternoon, Ms. Fielding. Today you are going to watch some video clips. Your task is to select which individual is telling the truth."

I turned to the surveillance camera. "Seriously, Dr. Corbin? You know I'm not going to do this."

"If you fail," Jeff continued to read, "you will be shocked with a Taser. We would like you to know that the Tasers we're using are old police Tasers that allow only one five-second shot per cartridge. I have an identical one here for you." He reached into the bag and tossed me a Taser. Behind him, the other security guy startled.

I caught the Taser in my cuffed hands. It reminded me of a cartoon version of a handgun. The right shape, more or less, but bigger and blockier.

Jeff tapped the bag. "We have additional cartridges for our Tasers, but whatever your responses to the questions, this experiment will not require us to deliver more than three shocks to you. I hereby assure you that even in the unfortunate event that you fail three times and conse"—he stumbled on the word—"*consequently* receive three shocks, they will cause no permanent damage to your body."

"Reassuring," I said.

"This experiment will thus simultaneously test your ability to assess another individual's truthfulness, and your willingness to accept and inflict pain. At this point, we invite you to ask any questions you might have about this experimental protocol." Jeff looked up from the paper he'd been reading from.

"No questions," I said, wrapping my hands around the barrel of the Taser. "Except . . . how do I fire this thing?"

"It's just like a gun," Jeff told me. "You point the barrel." He showed me the long end of the Taser. "And pull the trigger."

"So I could walk over and shoot him"—I waved at the other security guard with my Taser—"right now?"

"You can do whatever you want with your Taser," Jeff said. "But as I stated, each Taser has only one charge."

"Okay," I said. "So I get to shoot one of you once and you get to shoot me three times? That doesn't seem fair."

"No one has to shoot anyone. If you correctly identify the people who are telling the truth, no one gets Tasered."

I wondered if my Taser was even charged. Jeff and the other guard thought it was, that was clear to me, but Corbin had taken pains to not be in the room while the test was going on, and I was guessing that was in part so I couldn't get any hints from her face.

Of course, she also probably knew that, if she were in the room, I'd immediately shoot her, and then do my best to shove my Taser down her throat.

I pictured Corbin watching me from her office, itching for me to shoot someone. I put the Taser down on the table and primly folded my hands in front of me.

Jeff turned back to his script. "We're going to start by playing you three clips of senators saying they had no idea the Department was involved in the project with which you were so"—he hesitated at another unfamiliar word—"intimately connected. Tell us which senator is telling the truth."

After a moment, someone who was watching remotely—Dr. Corbin, or maybe some assistant mad scientist—started a video playing on the big monitor at the end of the room.

Three old men came on the screen, one after the other, each proclaiming their outrage at the Innocence Treatment. The first two were obviously lying. The third, a white man with a quavery voice, was telling the truth about his ignorance, though possibly that was just because he was so old he'd forgotten being informed about the project.

I looked straight at the camera. "Gosh, that's tough," I said. "I guess I'll go with the first guy."

Jeff shook his head, listening to his earbud. "I'm sorry," he told me. "That's incorrect."

I bolted up, leaving my Taser on the table, and stepped toward the orderly with the unbuttoned holster. "What? No! Give me another chance."

The other security guy pulled his Taser from its holster. "Not so smug now, are you?"

I ducked behind a chair, putting me even closer to the male orderly. "It's not fair. You have to give me another chan—"

The guard took a few steps to one side and shot me with his Taser.

Let me tell you. Getting Tasered sucks. Two little barbs snake out from the Taser and puncture your skin. That stings. Then the Taser starts pumping electricity into you, and that hurts even more, like a combination of getting burned and having ants crawling all over your skin. The pain isn't the worst part, though. The worst part is the loss of control. The electricity, or whatever, confuses your brain's connection to your muscles, and you lose all control of your body. I did not like that feeling at all.

I found myself on the floor, one orderly on either side of me. As they helped me up, my arms spasmed against the male orderly, lingering on the side of his belt. I collapsed back to the ground, hunching myself around the Taser I'd stolen from the orderly.

"Get her back in her seat," Jeff told them. The other security guard was scowling at the floor, and I had a vague memory of Jeff scolding him while I had been convulsing on the ground. Apparently, Jeff was supposed to give the order before I got shot.

They helped me back to my seat, still curled into a ball.

After a minute or two, Jeff said, "We're going to play you another three clips. Same deal—tell us who's lying."

This time it was Departmental officials. These were more interesting, seeing the way they were sweating, the genuine fear in their eyes. These were powerful people, two men and one woman who had spent much of the last ten years running the most powerful organization in the country, maybe in the world. And here they were, wriggling in front of the almost-unmuzzled press, bloggers and reporters sticking to the same respectful tones as usual, but their questions getting increasingly blunt.

The small part of my brain not preoccupied with Tasers and the location and stance of each guard and orderly wondered why Dr. Corbin had wanted me to see all this. To scare me? To congratulate me? It wasn't just random, that much was clear.

The woman in the video was telling the truth, or something close to it, with vague generalizations about exploratory research projects, while the two men who stubbornly maintained that the Department had known nothing about the Innocence Treatment were obviously lying. I glanced over at the security guy who had shot me. "Have you ever been Tasered?" I asked him.

"Ms. Fielding," Jeff said. "Let's stick to the matter at hand. Who was telling the truth this time?"

I took a deep breath, closing my hand around the Taser's grip, willing my hands to stop shaking. I knew that Corbin had given me the Taser, that I was probably doing exactly what she wanted. Still, I couldn't resist.

"Yes or no?" I asked the other security guy.

He stared back at me, saying nothing.

"If you don't answer me," Jeff said calmly, "I've been told to Taser you in ten seconds."

It would have been much easier if it wasn't for the damn

handcuffs. With the handcuffs on, I had to leave the stolen Taser in my lap, as I needed both hands to hold the one they'd given me.

I pointed the Taser they'd given me at the other security guy.

"You trying to scare me?" he said stoically. "Tasers don't scare me."

"Ten," Jeff said. "Nine. Eight. Seven. Six." On six he drew his Taser, and I shot him. My Taser worked just fine. He fell back in his seat, shaking. I had five seconds to get to his Taser.

Five. I dropped my Taser. The other security guard was in no hurry, casually taking his reloaded weapon from his holster.

Four. I picked up the Taser I'd stolen from the medical orderly.

Three. I shot the other security guard in the chest, peripherally noting the medical orderlies staring at me, the male orderly only now realizing I had his Taser, the woman orderly belatedly scrabbling at her own holstered weapon.

Two. I gathered my uncuffed legs beneath me and skidded over the tabletop on my butt.

One. The current coursing into Jeff cut off. I put my hands around Jeff's shaking hands and pointed his weapon at the woman orderly just now bringing her Taser to bear. I shot her.

Then, hopping off the table, I grabbed one of the heavy chairs. Bringing it over my head, I bashed it against the surveillance camera with all my strength. On the first hit, the little glass dome cracked. Two more hits, and I could see the camera beneath the dome. Another three hits and all that was left was wiring.

Around then the door opened. Four more security guards poured into the room. I dropped the chair and held up my empty hands.

Behind me, Jeff cursed softly. Then he said, "Would you care to take a guess now, Ms. Fielding? Which of those officials was telling the truth?"

"The woman." I walked back to the table. "And it's not a guess, Jeff. You know what else?"

The other security guard was just sitting up from where he'd toppled onto the ground. I pointed at him. "Your little friend is reporting everything that happens here to someone else. Probably the Department, but maybe some other corporation. He has *spy* written all over him."

Jeff turned to one of the guys who had just burst into the room. "My earbud is fried. Ask the boss what she wants us to do."

The security guard sitting on the floor—the guy I'd fingered as a corporate spy—said, "Hey, Jeff. You know she's lying, right?"

"Shut up," Jeff said.

And that was my afternoon. Honestly, it was a lot more fun than talking to poor Dr. Brechel.

FROM THE PRISON JOURNAL OF LAUREN C. FIELDING

I don't know how much time I have to write this. It could be less than an hour. It could be a day or two. No more, I'm sure. At some point soon the guards will unlock my door and escort me downstairs to where a Departmental van will whisk me off to . . . I don't know where. One of their not-so-secret facilities where enemies of the state are detained. Or maybe just a landfill where they can dump my body. Yesterday Dr. Corbin told me the Departmental prison will make this place look like a country club, and in that, at least, I think she's telling the truth.

I'm writing this furiously in hopes that I'll be able to hand this journal to someone in the detention center . . . on the off chance that they take me to a detention center rather than, say, a landfill. On the even tinier chance that someone will get it out and make it public. Probably a sign of my continuing naïveté that I'm even considering such a series of long shots. But at this point, hope is all I have. Maybe Dr. Brechel and I aren't so different after all.

Speaking of Dr. Brechel, it's been four days since the last time I saw him. Three days since the fun with the Tasers. Assuming they've been turning on and off the lights in a pattern that's reasonably close to sunrise and sunset in the outside world. As I lie awake in the darkness, it's occurred to me that Corbin could be messing with that, too. Maybe it's actually two in the afternoon and that's why I can't fall asleep. Maybe the reason I didn't feel like eating anything at dinner is that they've been bringing me my meals every two hours.

I didn't realize how much my meetings with Dr. Brechel helped me structure my days until I stopped meeting with him. The only thing keeping me sane now is exercise. Two days ago I managed to do ten handstand push-ups in a row for the first time.

Yesterday morning I was in the midst of a set of regular push-ups when my door opened a crack and the big guard, Jeff, put a bag of clothes on the floor inside the room. "Good morning, Ms. Fielding. Dr. Corbin is ready to see you today. She thought you might appreciate some new clothes to wear."

Since I got here, I've been wearing a pair of those green cotton pajamas they give to hospital patients. I only had the one outfit with me when I came into Paxeon custody, and that got some blood on it during my reunion with Eric the orderly. Still, I wasn't interested in dressing up for Corbin.

I looked back at the floor and kept going with my push-ups. Fifty-four. Fifty-five.

Jeff hesitated. "She also asked you to shower."

Fifty-six. Fity-seven. Fifty-eight.

"I showered yesterday," I said, pleased that I wasn't short of breath. Fifty-nine. Sixty.

"If you don't take a shower and dress yourself," Jeff said, "she's told us to help the orderlies bathe you and get you dressed. By force, if we have to. None of us want to, but you understand we all need our jobs, right?"

Sixty-one. Sixty-two.

The door opened farther and he stepped inside. I eyed him out of my peripheral vision. He stood with his legs apart, one hand on his Taser's handle. Even without his Taser, he easily had a hundred pounds on me, all of it muscle. And even if I could get past him, there was another big security guy a few steps behind him—not the same guy who'd been with him the other day, by the way.

"Look," Jeff said. "No hard feelings about what happened with the Taser. You're an impressive kid. Seriously."

I went back to my push-ups. Sixty-three. Sixty-four.

Jeff relaxed a little, though he left his hand on his Taser. "So I'm asking you as nice as I know how: Please. Please take the damn shower by yourself. Get yourself dressed. All of us will have a much better day."

I thought about it. Thought about how Dr. Corbin would probably enjoy watching me fight, would enjoy seeing me forcibly bathed. "Okay," I said. "Give me twenty minutes and I'll be ready."

He nodded and backed out the door.

I went back to my push-ups, but once I got to one hundred, I took a shower and put on the clothes Dr. Corbin had sent me. A long-sleeved blouse and jeans. Nice clean underwear and a bra. All of which would have fit me perfectly a few months ago. I've lost a lot of weight since the operation. Riley would be so jealous. I wonder what Riley and Gabriella think has happened to me. I wonder if they've read my journal entries. If so, I hope they get that I appreciated them again by the end.

I knocked on the door to my room when I was done. Jeff and the other security guy were waiting for me. I stood there while they cuffed my hands and my ankles, then shuffled after them as they led me toward the elevator.

Dr. Corbin's office is on the top floor of the Paxeon building. I remember visiting her with my parents, staring out the huge windows at the distant mountains, so certain that everyone had my best interests at heart that I didn't bother paying attention to the conversation.

Corbin was sitting behind her desk when we arrived.

She looked up when the door opened, smiled, and came around her desk to take my handcuffed hands in her hands. "Lauren!" Her genuine pleasure at seeing me was creepier than fake pleasure would have been. "It's so nice to see you. I would have visited you earlier but, you understand, I didn't want to throw off your various indicators, not when Dr. Brechel was working so hard to establish them."

"Indicators?"

She dismissed my question with one hand. "Nothing that need concern you now. I've satisfied myself that your condition's stable—that's the important thing."

"What happened to Dr. Brechel?" I asked.

Her eyes shifted up to the ceiling. "You know—I'm not entirely sure."

"How can you not be sure? Did you kill him or just fire him?"

"*I*"—she emphasized the word—"did nothing to Dr. Brechel."

"Is he alive?"

"I doubt it," she said, looking mildly bemused, as though I was pestering her about something that had nothing to do with her. "I think he got himself into some trouble. Listen, Lauren. I want to offer you a job."

"Yeah right. And what happens when I 'get myself into some trouble'?"

She chuckled. "Unlike Brechel, you have the sense to stay out of trouble. And, besides, you will be far more useful than Dr. Brechel, so trouble will avoid you."

"Useful," I said. "How so?"

"A beautiful young woman, uncannily perceptive, and with no restraint on her violent tendencies . . . You could be a very valuable member of my team."

"I don't buy it. Why don't you just turn me stupid again already?"

Corbin surprised me. "We tried, sweetheart. We gave you a complete dose of the Innocence Treatment the day you came back to us. Since then, we've exposed you to it half a dozen times. The last time we gave you"—she thought for a moment—"about ten times the dose it would take to turn an ordinary person of your weight into the most easily led idiot you can imagine for at least a few weeks, if not a few months. None of the doses had any impact that we could measure. That was where Dr. Brechel was so useful— if the treatment had any impact at all, it would certainly have become apparent in your sessions with him."

Oh. Suddenly things made a little more sense. "That's why I'm still alive."

Corbin made a face. "Puh-leeze. I never intended to kill you. But yes, your immunity to the Innocence Treatment is one more reason you'd be a great addition to my team. You'd have to grow your hair out, or wear a wig if you prefer, but beyond that, I think you're ready to go into the field. Your personality profile, your skill set. It's all perfect."

"You had me seeing a shrink twice a day for the last three weeks to change my personality profile."

Again she chuckled a little. She was genuinely enjoying our conversation. "Don't be ridiculous. We both know that wasn't why I hired Brechel. I had to make sure your condition was stable, that's all. Imagine if we hired you only to find you no longer wanted to hurt people. Or, say, you were no longer good at reading strangers. Dr. Brechel assured us your paranoid tendencies are extremely stable. He was very confident.

"And then your performance a few days ago." She kissed her fingers. "Beautiful. Handcuffed, you Tasered three people, including two very well-trained soldiers . . . and a completely harmless medical orderly." She grinned and shook her head, every inch the proud parent. "All that for no reason aside from you felt like it. In fact, unless I very much miss my guess, you tried to resist, but you simply couldn't restrain yourself."

"You liked that, did you?"

"I . . . appreciated it. Lauren, we're here today because I want to offer you a job. Not just a job, a life. A much longer life than the one that otherwise faces you. All you have to do is what you want to do anyway. Hurt people who anger you. Reveal liars and spies. You'll get very rich in the process."

"What did you do to Brechel?" I asked.

"*I* did nothing. Brechel killed himself," Corbin said. "No one made the idiot threaten the Department. He sent a copy of your case notes to some higher-ups in the Department, along with a warning that they'd be posted online if he died."

"Oh," I said, feeling sick. "I told him to be discreet."

"I know you did, sweetheart. I saw the video. You can't blame yourself." She shrugged airily. "You can imagine how his threats went over with the big guns at the Department. They care far less about exposure than they do about being threatened by a podunk subcontractor. Especially now, when everyone can smell the Department's blood in the water. One sign of weakness and the piranhas will swarm.

"But enough about Brechel. You have to decide if you want to leave this compound with me or be handed over to the Department. Whatever's left of it, I mean, with the top dogs jumping ship like rats from a sinking Emergency Act." She chuckled at her own words.

"I never expected to leave," I said.

"I don't care about your *expectations*. I can use you." She tapped her mobile device. "I just got a message from a contact in West Africa—one of their native foremen has been pilfering diamonds for months. You could go there for a few days and find the culprit. Or, if that's too far from home, something similar in Canada where some of the aboriginal tribes keep blowing up the oil pipelines in the north. The Department has a strong hunch that some sympathizers in the Canadian military are turning a blind eye to the terrorists. Passing on kill-switch sequences and so on. You could settle that."

"So what? We'd just let bygones be bygones?" I said. "I'd go to work for the Department?"

"Of course not," she said. "The Department will never forgive you. We'd feign your death and you'd come to work for me. I have new identity papers all lined up."

"The Department would never forgive me but you will? Just like that?"

"I have nothing to forgive, sweetheart." Corbin smiled the broadest smile I've ever seen from her. It was the first time I noticed her teeth, which are absurdly perfect—obviously the result of some expensive surgery. She saw me looking and her left hand twitched toward her mouth. I could suddenly picture her when she was my age. Brilliant but awkward, a scholarship student at the most expensive schools, concealing her horrible teeth from her wealthy friends. Driven to succeed at all costs. Show the snobs that she was smarter, tougher, better than they'd ever be.

It annoyed me, the sudden insight and the sympathy it gave me for her. It's not like she was some pathetic poor girl now. She stood there beaming at me, and I had never found her so frightening. Because I had no idea why she was so happy.

"You somehow edited my journal before it was released, didn't you? Took your name out of it?"

She shook her head, still grinning. "Perish the thought. Your little journal entries were released exactly as you wrote them." I stared at her face, and I was positive—as positive as I've ever been about anything—that she was telling the truth. Either they've made me an idiot who will believe anything again, or Dr. Corbin was genuinely happy about the fact that I exposed her scheme to the world.

"Thanks to you, the world knows all about the Innocence Treatment. Not just that—it's come out that the Department exposed several United States senators to the treatment, hoping to change their minds on the Emergency Act. Once this became public, there was widespread outrage throughout Congress, some of it actually authentic. All talk of extending the Emergency Act ended."

She stopped smiling for an instant, putting a look of mock horror on her face. "And obviously I was shocked, deeply shocked, at the discovery that the Department had used *my* research to meddle with the brains of elected officials in the United States. I had no idea that was what the Department intended. In fact, I've left my position with the Paxeon corporation as a result of this shocking revelation. Effective as of next week."

She let the grin slide back onto her face. "Which is not to say I won't continue to supply certain services and products to the Department. As it happens, all the patents that resulted from my most important work were filed in my name. Paxeon is facing legal action from several quarters and, with any luck, the corporation will be driven into bankruptcy soon. It will be years before anyone can mount a serious challenge to my intellectual property. Also, oddly enough, the details of my most successful and experimental procedure have all gone missing from the Department's database, something that no one there can quite explain."

I kept my face blank, not wanting to give her the satisfaction. Not that it was such a big surprise that Sasha had been working for her, but still . . . I felt something inside of me die. Maybe one last bit of the old, hopeful Lauren.

"And I haven't even mentioned the publicity." She shook her head. "Money cannot buy the kind of publicity your 'exposé' has gotten me . . . Every time a powerful person has made a mistake in the past month, it's been attributed to our treatment. People are very interested in getting access to the Innocence Treatment. Some extremely rich people, along with their associated corporate interests. Not to mention some extremely wealthy foreign countries. And thanks to your journal entries, they know exactly where to get it."

It's funny in a way. There I was—little Miss Perceptive, lecturing Dr. Brechel about how I see things as they are and not just how I want them to be. And still, Corbin's betrayal of the Department caught me completely off guard. I stared at her for a few seconds.

"Dear girl." She patted my cheek. "Surely you can see that I am in your debt. Thanks to you the world knows what I can do. Which brings me back to my proposal to you: imagine us as a team, Lauren. You're the one person in the world who's immune to the treatment that I'm selling. Let's say the CEO of some corporation is annoying someone. You can take a swig of some treated, but still very nice wine, then offer it to him. He thinks, 'No one would deliberately expose themselves to the Innocence Treatment. If they did, they certainly wouldn't be able to lie about it.' He takes a drink and off you go."

"Was this your plan all along?" I said. "If I hadn't released my own journals would you have released them yourself?"

She shrugged. "Let's just say, whatever happened, I was bound to come out ahead. The business journals call it 'positive structuring.' "

"But why would you trust me to work for you?" I said.

"*Trust* you?" Corbin rolled her eyes. "Have you ever noticed that it's only the weakest people who are concerned with trust? You want to know what I trust? I trust that you're smart, and I trust you to pursue your own best interests. As your manager, my job will be to make sure your interests line up with mine."

I looked at her closely. There was something she knew that I didn't know. Something she couldn't wait to tell me. "What?" I said. "Go ahead and tell me. I know you want to."

"Ah. You *are* good. I *have* been looking forward to introducing you to the manager of field operations at my new company." She pressed a button on her desk. An old-fashioned intercom—I'd seen them in movies, but never in real life before.

I could tell—for all the good it did me, which was none at all—how much she enjoyed the theatricality of leaning toward the intercom and purring smoothly into it: "We're ready for Mr. Adams now."

I didn't need to turn toward the door to know who was going to walk in. But I turned around anyway. I couldn't help myself.

So I was staring at the door when Sasha walked in, wearing the same rumpled jeans and faded T-shirt as usual. No glasses though. He smiled at Dr. Corbin and squeezed my shoulder. "Hey," he said.

"Tell her," Dr. Corbin said eagerly.

"She knows," Sasha said. "She heard you say 'We're ready for Mr. Adams.' Plus, she heard you gloating about how the Department doesn't have the records on the Innocence Treatment anymore."

"Tell her," Dr. Corbin repeated, smiling a little.

"You're a drama queen, you know that?" Sasha turned to me. "You wanna say it yourself? You must have figured it out a few minutes ago, if not earlier."

I looked back and forth between the two of them, hardly paying attention to his words. It was the rapport he had with Corbin. The common affection. He wasn't faking it. He liked her and she liked him—it was the most genuine emotion I'd ever seen from her—the little crinkle around her eyes when she looked at him, the slightest turn-up of one side of her lips.

"You had a side contract with Corbin," I said. "That's why you deleted the files on me. That's why you helped me break into the system." I tried to remember whose idea it had been to break into the Department's database in the first place. It had been mine, hadn't it? "You were on her side all along."

Sasha nodded. "Well. Yeah. I hope you're not expecting me to feel guilty. You're the one who blogged about my betrayal of the Department to the whole frigging world."

"I warned you," I said.

"Oh, yeah. That was really generous of you." His face took on a mock-sorrowful expression and he imitated my voice. " 'Um, hey, Sasha, listen. I'm going to get the Department super-pissed at you. You have four weeks to figure out a way to not get killed or deported.' "

"They had my sister."

"You know what?" I heard a strain of real anger in his voice. "Your sister made her own decisions. You warned her, but she had to keep hanging out with her loser friends and visiting 'activist' websites. There's a ridiculous phrase—'activist website.' Sitting in your parents' home writing secret messages to other spoiled middle-class kids does not make you an activist."

"Sasha," Dr. Corbin said indulgently. "You're supposed to be convincing her to join our team, not insulting her sister."

"I'm appreciating his honesty," I said. "Finally." I stared at Sasha's face. "Did I ever mean anything to you?"

"Of course," he said. "You still do. Just not quite as much as staying alive and free means to me."

"You're not free. You've just got a new boss, that's all."

"Everyone works for someone, Lauren. I sure feel free." He tapped his eyes. "You notice I'm not wearing glasses? I got the eye operation the day I left the Department. And I don't have to wear camera-enabled glasses anymore. These days when I go to the bathroom, I don't have to worry about some Department bureaucrat seeing my junk if I look down before zipping up."

He looked at my face and his voice softened. "I'm sorry I couldn't tell you about this before, but we couldn't risk it. What if the Department asked you some questions before handing you to Patricia, you know?"

Corbin nodded and leaned toward me. "Join us, Lauren. Don't you want your skills to be used?"

Sasha sighed. "Are you *trying* to sound like Darth Vader, Patricia?" He did this deep breathy thing and said, "Luke, join the dark side. Embrace your anger."

Corbin laughed, but Sasha must have seen the confusion in my eyes. "Star Wars?" he asked.

I shook my head.

"Stupid Department trainers," he said. "Making us watch stuff that no actual kid has watched for years. Look. This isn't a big deal. It's a job, that's all. You agree to work for her, and Patricia gives you a new identity. You don't want to end up in the Department's custody. They are not happy with you."

I'm not saying it wasn't tempting. I don't want to die. And the thought of being with Sasha indefinitely . . . of course I liked it. But sugarcoat it as they would, all their jobs would be for the wrong side. Because it's always the wrong side that's willing to pay someone like Dr. Corbin.

"I'm not interested in joining your team," I said. I kept my face expressionless and my voice light. I didn't want Sasha or Corbin to see what this conversation was doing to me. I couldn't believe Sasha was going along with Corbin. I had always thought . . . I had always *hoped* that there was something more to Sasha. "Thanks, though."

As for why I didn't go along with Corbin just long enough to get free of the prison, I . . . It's complicated. I've been thinking a lot about this kind of thing since I turned myself in to Paxeon. It seems to me that no one sets out to work for the bad guys. Not Brechel, not Sasha. Not the big guard, Jeff. Maybe not even Dr. Corbin. They'd just made the compromises they thought they had to. Then, all of a sudden, there they were, informing on their friends or interrogating a political prisoner. I wasn't going down that path.

Sasha took a few steps until he was standing immediately before my chair. "Let's take her out of her restraints," he said to Dr. Corbin. "I want her to feel a little free before she decides."

"I've decided," I said. "I will never work for her."

They both ignored me. Sasha got the key from the guard. He took off the handcuffs and ankle cuffs. He squatted before me and gently massaged the skin around my ankles.

I couldn't resist. I stood up and stretched.

Sasha stepped closer to me and looked into my eyes. "Lauren," he said quietly. "Please. What we had—what we have—it's great. It's wonderful. But if you think we can go on like that without someone who can protect us from the Department . . ."—he took a deep breath, bit his thumbnail, and shook his head—"don't kid yourself."

The restraints were off me and I was just a few inches from him. I could have severely hurt him, maybe even killed him before the guards could have gotten to me.

I put my hands on his shoulders. "What if I *want* to kid myself?" I leaned forward and kissed him.

FROM THE PRISON JOURNAL
OF LAUREN C. FIELDING

December 17, 2031

I'd like to tell you I kissed Sasha because I could tell he was really on my side. That it was part of some master plan Sasha and I had worked out before I went into custody, or even that I was trying to seduce him into helping me, or at least into feeling bad about his betrayal of me. But none of that's true.

To the extent that I was thinking anything at all it was something like this: *If I'm going to be killed in the near future, I want at least one more kiss. And Sasha is a truly gifted kisser.*

Standing there in that enormous sunlit office with that horrible little woman and the two guards in the doorway, it took Sasha maybe half a second to start kissing me back. His breath tasted like soy sauce and water and . . . metal. He had a metal object in his mouth that he was pushing into my mouth with his tongue.

I pushed the metal object to the inside of one cheek and kept kissing him, pulling his hips closer to me as he squeezed me closer to him. Honestly, if Dr. Corbin and the guards hadn't been in the room, I'm thinking there was a good chance that we would have shucked our clothes right there and then, surveillance cameras be damned.

But Dr. Corbin stood a few feet away, watching, her mouth slightly open, which was enough to put a damper on anyone's sexual feelings.

After a few more seconds Sasha pulled away. "That change your mind?"

I smiled without showing my teeth. Shook my head.

"You'd rather die than work with me?" Sasha said.

I half shrugged, not wanting to open my mouth and risk revealing whatever it was Sasha had slipped to me.

Dr. Corbin motioned Sasha out of the room, a look of genuine sadness on her face. "You're still so naïve," she said as the guards were cuffing me. "Would it be so bad to be on the winning team for once? This place is a country club compared to the prison where the Department is going to stick you. If you're lucky. More likely they'll just take you to a field somewhere and kill you. Please, Lauren."

In a movie, I'd have responded with some final words about freedom, and how if futile resistance was my only choice, I'd prefer futile resistance to doing her dirty work. But in real life, when you have a metal thing in your mouth that you don't want someone noticing, you don't talk back. Instead I just stared at the wall behind her and worked on getting the whatever-it-was lodged securely between my teeth and cheek. Then I waited. Waited until they got my cuffs back on and I'd shuffled back to my room. Waited until they got my cuffs off and locked the door. Waited until I could turn my head away from the video camera. Only then, pretending that I was sneezing, did I spit the object into my right hand. And found . . .

A key to the handcuffs. The key Sasha borrowed from the guard and forgot to give back. Pretty cocky of Sasha, if you think about it. He must have put the key in his mouth as soon as he unlocked my cuffs—that's how confident he was that I was going to kiss him, or at least let him kiss me.

The key, by the way, is why I stopped my last journal entry where I did. I didn't want there to be any chance that Corbin would read about the key before I'd had a chance to use it. The key was useless as long as I was locked in my room on the seventh floor.

My chance came the following morning, when Corbin—cutting her losses, I guess, or maybe under pressure from her friends at the Department—decided to turn me over. Jeff and another guard picked me up in my room after breakfast.

I was in the elevator with the guards when I asked, "How long is the ride to the Department prison?"

The guards exchanged glances. No doubt they both knew there was a fair chance I'd never make it to any prison. Jeff answered, "We don't know. Sorry."

"Could I use the bathroom one more time?" I asked. "You can leave the cuffs on me. I just really have to go." I blushed a little.

"There's a women's bathroom on the ground floor next to the elevator."

I'd been in this particular bathroom a few times on my early visits to Paxeon. I remembered a high but wide window, streaming sunlight over the sink area.

Jeff and the other guy exchanged glances again. "Okay," Jeff said. "No problem."

The elevator doors opened and we walked down the hallway together. Jeff knocked on the door to the women's bathroom. "Anyone in there?" he called. There was no answer. He did a quick sweep of the bathroom, then motioned me in.

He stood in front of the stall while the other guard stayed in the hallway, I suppose to make sure no potential rescuer tried to swoop in. Or maybe just because he felt weird about going into a women's bathroom.

I sat on the toilet seat and peed as I quietly unlocked first my handcuffs, then my ankle cuffs. I pulled up my pants, buttoned them, and crouched down to look at Jeff's feet. He was turned to one side, facing the door to the bathroom. I threw the handcuffs behind him against the back wall of the bathroom. Jeff immediately spun around and took a step in that direction.

Given Jeff's size, not to mention the guy waiting in the hallway, I figured I had one chance. I slipped through the stall door and leaped onto Jeff's back, hooking my arm around his neck in the most aggressive choke hold I knew. Benitez never let us practice choke holds, but he demonstrated them once in a while. I remembered him saying that, done correctly, this one would take ten seconds to knock someone out, and about another ten seconds to kill them.

Jeff wasted a few seconds going for his Taser. I had my legs wrapped around his waist, and my thighs were stronger than his hands. Then he tried slamming me against the wall, but the sinks got in his way. By then he was already weakening.

He punched at my face twice feebly, then sagged to the floor. I counted another three seconds before letting go.

Then, standing on the sink closest to the wall, I pulled the window as far open as it went. Not that far. It was one of those slant-open windows that don't open more than a foot or two at their widest. I pulled myself up on the windowsill, lay flat, and wiggled toward the opening.

Six months ago I never would have fit through. Yesterday I managed it, though I did get a nasty scrape on my right hip as I squeezed out the window. I dropped softly to the concrete parking lot outside.

I found myself . . . screwed. Standing at the edge of a massive parking lot. Freezing cold, without even a sweater to keep me warm. The only thing visible was a secured highway in the distance. Even if I knew how to steal a car, I had no idea how to drive. A few hundred feet away, I saw a black Department van waiting for me at the main entrance of the Paxeon building. I started to creep through the parking lot, keeping down, intent on at least making it out of the Paxeon compound. If I could get to a residential neighborhood maybe I could break into someone's house, steal some clothes and food. If nothing else, I could get my story out.

I heard a car slowly cruising around the Paxeon building. It eased to a stop under the window I'd just come through. I darted between two parked cars and lay flat on the cold pavement, listening to the car come closer. I heard it turn down the nearest aisle— the same one I'd been making my way along. I wriggled beneath one of the parked cars, a green minivan.

The car stopped a few yards away from me. I heard a car door opening and I caught the strong smell of French fries.

"I was planning on throwing my life away in a brave but doomed attempt to rescue you," Sasha said. "But this is probably a better idea."

I rolled out from under the minivan and glanced up. Sasha was in the driver's seat, looking at me through his open passenger door. He met my eyes, not quite smiling. "Hey. You want a ride?"

EPILOGUE

Dear Reader,

You're probably wondering: what happened next? The short—and *almost* entirely true—answer is, I have no idea.

The Department has done everything it can do, and it can do a lot, to erase all evidence that Lauren ever existed. That effort probably saved my life during the bloodiest part of the second uprising (why send someone to kill the sister of a girl who never existed?), but it has made it very difficult to find out anything certain about Lauren's whereabouts in recent years. Even Lauren's original journal entries are getting harder to find online due to the Department's efforts. (Which, in fact, is one of the primary reasons I decided to work on this book.)

Dr. Corbin was almost certainly executed by the Department. They arrested her two years after the events detailed in Lauren's journal, in the very early days of the second uprising. A few days after her arrest, they announced her "suicide." I have no idea why they killed her, nor if it had anything to do with the Innocence Treatment. I have no idea if Lauren was involved.

All this is true, but it's not entirely satisfying, is it? You know, or at least those of you who are paying attention must strongly suspect, that I've had some contact with Lauren over the years. How else did I get those final five journal entries?

It is tempting to simply tell a lie here. Though the Department has been purged and transformed at least three times in the last decade, I have no doubt that many people who remain in power mean Lauren (and anyone associated with her) ill.

But in the interest of partially repaying my debt to my sister, I'll be honest.

I genuinely have no idea what Lauren has been doing, nor where she's been living for the last decade. However, I have seen her twice in person since we said goodbye in the aisle of that airplane. Once was on the day I graduated from university. I was walking across the stage to collect my diploma when I glanced out and saw Lauren smiling in the audience. By the time I made my way to where she'd been sitting, she was gone.

On the other occasion, I was sitting on a beach on the east coast of Spain, a few kilometers south of Barcelona. It was my first vacation in years, meant to celebrate the publication of my first book.[20]

---

[20] E. Sofia Fielding, *Gilded Brutalism: Modernist Poetry and the Communist Revolution in China* (Oxford: Oxford University Press, 2038), 296 pp.

I'd taken the train from the Barcelona city center to the most perfect beach I've ever seen, before or since. Some magic of mineral sediment made the water of the Balearic Sea look speckled with gold and the people on the beach were uniformly young, half-naked, and perfectly formed. A bit sun-drunk, I was watching a beautiful teenaged couple hit a ball back and forth with wooden rackets when a young woman in a bikini, sunglasses, and a wide-brimmed sun hat approached me.

" 'Scuse me. Can I borrow your sunscreen?" she asked in American-accented English.

"Sure," I said automatically, reaching for my sunscreen before my gaze snapped back to her.

"Hand me the sunscreen," Lauren said calmly.

I gave her the sunscreen, and she squirted some onto her hands and began rubbing it onto her chest.

"True fact," she said. "Even in this day and age, most surveillance footage is reviewed by men. Funny, isn't it? A ton of studies have shown men are worse at it than women. Not to mention more easily distracted." She slowly rubbed sunscreen on her thighs and winked at me. "Not that I think we're being surveilled," she said. "But you can't be too careful, right? I've pissed some people off."

I stared at her. She looked . . . great. Beautiful. Happy. Grown-up.

Her lips twisted into the full-wattage smile I remembered. My little sister's grin. "Not what people expect me to look like, right? Kind of funny—as though I'd have to walk around bald and skinny and full of angst for the rest of my life." She shook her head. "Speaking of which, did you see the girl who played me in that movie? How hard could she possibly punch someone with arms that skinny?"

"I don't watch movies about you," I said.

"Probably a good idea," she said. "They made you super-prissy."

"Where have you been, Lauren? Who have you pissed off?"

"Only people who deserved it." Then, more seriously, "I hear you're writing a book about me."

"How the . . . How did you hear that?" I'd been going back and forth with the big aggregators for months by then, trying to sell one of them on the idea of producing the definitive version of Lauren's journals. But there'd been no public announcement. There'd been no contract. At that point, there hadn't even been a phone conversation. "If you don't want me to, I won't—"

"Of course I want you to," she said. "That movie ending was ridiculous. As though Sasha and I would let ourselves get cornered in some ugly highway rest stop. In New Jersey of all places. What would we be doing in New Jersey?"

"What would you be doing anywhere?" I asked. "Where do you live?"

She looked over her sunglasses and met my eyes. I had a sudden memory of staring into her eyes when she was a kid. Her eyes are a hard-to-pin-down shade of hazel, and she used to periodically walk up to me and ask: "What color are my eyes today,

Ev?" Today they looked greenish gray, shrewd and loving all at once.

"Better you don't know," she said gently. Something in the distance caught her attention and she shifted her weight toward me, putting her hand on my shoulder. "I should go." Her hand felt calloused and hard, completely out of keeping with the flowered pink bikini she was wearing. "You'll find some old journal entries of mine in your beach bag. Tell Mom and Dad I send my love." She leaned toward me and kissed my cheeks—first one, then the other. Just one Spanish woman saying goodbye to another. "Love you."

She strode off, and vanished into the crowd of half-naked, tanned young people. Half a minute later I couldn't have found her if I'd wanted to.

Maybe ten minutes after she left, a half dozen men, sweltering in desert camouflage uniforms and carrying assault rifles, jogged past my towel. They didn't slow as they passed me. It probably had nothing to do with Lauren, but after they had vanished in the distance, I walked back to my hotel as quickly as I could. I didn't mention seeing Lauren when I videoed my boyfriend that evening. Didn't even give my parents her message until I saw them in person when I was back in the UK.

And that's been it for my in-person interactions with my sister over the last decade. I get a message from her once, maybe twice a year. Never in a way that gives a hint of her current location. A text from an anonymized IP address congratulating me when I got engaged. Flowers for our mother when she was diagnosed with liver cancer. Never any ongoing contact. Never any way to ask her questions.

I understand, of course. If I was in touch with her, people could threaten her through me. But still, I wish I knew where she was. I wish I knew if she was okay.

Honestly, there's a part of me that wishes Lauren had just stayed the way she was. Innocent as she was, Lauren was the best person I've ever met.

That said, I've read her journal entries hundreds of times and I think Dr. Corbin was right when, in that last meeting, she told Lauren she was still naïve. Anyone who fights the system as hard as Lauren does is still, deep down, an innocent. Because we all know the system wins eventually, right?

Sometimes I think I know the answer to that. Sometimes, I'm not so sure.

Dr. E. Sofia Fielding, Ph.D.
London, UK
June 2041

ACKNOWLEDGMENTS

Thank you to the Canada Council for the Arts for their generous support of my writing—in particular for the 2015 Grant for Professional Writers (Creative Writing Program).

A special thanks to all the friends and family who read and critiqued early drafts of this novel: Linda DeMeulemeester, Tamar Goelman, Sarah Eisenstein, Jessica Woolliams, and Susan Yi. Janine Cross didn't read this one in draft, but the monthly writing group meetings that she, Linda, and I shared were like a drumbeat that kept me writing. Benjamin Rosenbaum didn't read this one, either, but he did contribute some very useful thoughts on social hacking.

Thanks to my editor, Katherine Jacobs, and the rest of the crew at Roaring Brook Press for their inspiring and intelligent suggestions. This book is tighter, smarter, and better than it would have been without you.

Thanks to Lindsay Ribar for her faith in my writing, her feedback on this novel, and for making the connection to Kate. Thanks to Wendi Gu for her hard work in taking over when Lindsay left.

Debbie—thanks for being patient and waiting until after this was published to read it. Aitan, Marcie, and Don—you weren't quite as patient, but thanks for your enthusiasm!

Finally I want to thank my children. Every day you inspire me to tell more and better stories. (Except for sometimes at night when I get too tired, and just want all of us to fall asleep. Thanks for being cool with that, too.)